"Saturday Was a Mistake,"

Lee said with a catch in her voice.

"All of it?"

"All of it."

His eyes burned into her. "Okay, if that's how you see it. Let's make a few more mistakes."

"You just can't resist making clever cracks," she burst out furiously.

"On the contrary, I was making a very serious suggestion. What happened between us was out of this world." The look in his eyes was a soft, sensuous caress.

NANCY JOHN

has been a full-time writer since 1964. She likes to travel and research the backgrounds of her novels, whose settings she describes vividly. She and her husband of thirty years make their country home in Sussex, England, where they pursue their love of nature in the romantically beautiful English countryside.

Dear Reader:

SILHOUETTE DESIRE is an exciting new line of contemporary romances from Silhouette Books. During the past year, many Silhouette readers have written in telling us what other types of stories they'd like to read from Silhouette, and we've kept these comments and suggestions in mind in developing SILHOUETTE DESIRE.

DESIREs feature all of the elements you like to see in a romance, plus a more sensual, provocative story. So if you want to experience all the excitement, passion and joy of falling in love, then SILHOUETTE DESIRE is for you.

Karen Solem
Editor-in-Chief
Silhouette Books

NANCY JOHN
Night With A Stranger

Silhouette Desire
Published by Silhouette Books New York
America's Publisher of Contemporary Romance

SILHOUETTE BOOKS, a Division of Simon & Schuster, Inc.
1230 Avenue of the Americas, New York, N.Y. 10020

ISBN: 0-671-49356-6

First Silhouette Books printing February, 1984

10 9 8 7 6 5 4 3 2 1

Books by Nancy John

Silhouette Romance

Tormenting Flame #17
The Spanish House #34
To Trust Tomorrow #57
Outback Summer #85
A Man for Always #115
Make-Believe Bride #192
Window to Happiness #262

Silhouette Special Edition

So Many Tomorrows #17
Web of Passion #38
Summer Rhapsody #75
Never Too Late #106

Silhouette Desire

Night with a Stranger #119

1

~❦❦❦❦❦❦❦❦❦~

"Oh darn this rotten, stinking, horrible fog," Lee Jordan muttered to herself tensely. "Where the dickens have I got to?"

As her car lurched into yet another deep rut she reflected wretchedly that she seemed to have ended up in the middle of nowhere. Obviously, she had somehow branched off the moorland road through the mountains onto a narrow byway, and she'd only realized her mistake when going back was out of the question. There was no space to turn 'round between the rock-strewn grassy banks, and the thought of reversing into the blank white wall of fog behind her was too daunting. Even if she didn't run off the track, she'd be likely to collide with a straying sheep.

Three hours ago, soon after she'd set out from Bristol, she had heard on the car radio a warning of bad visibility in the Welsh mountains, but Lee had never dreamed that a September fog could be as thick as this. No more, she'd reasoned, than a slight hazing of the golden autumn sunshine which would require extra care in driving. So she'd pressed on. But a few miles back she'd found to her dismay that the drifts of mist which occasionally obscured the shape of oncoming vehicles had kept swirling and thickening around her until she was traveling in a solitary world of dense, wet whiteness. And somewhere she had stupidly taken that wrong fork.

Well, she only had herself to blame. The engine droned in low gear and she knew that she was steadily climbing higher. Perhaps high enough to get clear of the fog? she thought with a rush of hope. But the murky gloom ahead grew deeper, if anything, and early nightfall seemed inevitable.

Then she saw a glimmer of light, elusive as the glow of a will-o'-the-wisp. It vanished, but reappeared a moment later, beckoning to her like a beacon. She inched forward until there could be no possible doubt. The light resolved itself into the warmly comforting shape of a curtained window, though the rest of the building was still invisible to her.

Lee stopped the car and got out, pulling on her brown suede raincoat. Peering into the gloom, she made out the turn-in of a rough driveway. Following this, she was relieved to see the solid structure of a whitewashed cottage taking shape. From within came the muted sound of jazz music.

After stumbling against a pile of logs, she eventually found a door. There seemed to be no knocker, so she rapped on it with her knuckles. Getting no answer, she rapped again more loudly, and called out, "Hi, in there. Anybody home?"

Still no response. Feeling around carefully, Lee found a ringed handle, and when she turned it the door yielded— opening straight into a living room. Cautiously, she poked her head in and called again. But clearly the music was drowning out her voice. She slipped inside and quickly closed the door behind her to keep out the billowing fog.

The room, though cottage-plain, looked attractive and comfortable. It had white walls, and the low ceiling was supported by age-blackened oak beams; the floor was flagstoned, scattered with sheepskin rugs. There was a big cushioned sofa and a couple of armchairs, all covered in floral white cretonne, and an alcove contained an oval dining table and four wicker-seated, high-backed chairs. Nearby stood an oaken dresser with a selection of Welsh pottery on the shelves. Warm, orange-tinted light was provided by a pair of parchment-shaded bronze table lamps and, looking wonderfully inviting to Lee, there was a blazing log fire. Moreover, a mouth-watering aroma of cooking permeated the air, reminding her that she'd merely snatched a cheese-and-cracker sandwich for her Sunday lunch, expecting to dine well this evening when she reached the hotel.

With a click the record came to an end, and the sudden quiet was accentuated by a steady drip of water from the eaves. Then, as Lee was about to call out again, she heard the soft pad of footsteps. She swung 'round to see a man enter through an archway to her right, dressed merely in a short, white terry bathrobe, with his long legs bare and no shoes. For a few pulsing, electric moments they stared at one another in silence, then he slowly lowered the striped towel with which he'd been rubbing his teak-dark hair.

"Where the heck did you spring from?" he demanded, a grin breaking across his craggy features. "I was brought up not to believe in ghosts, but you're making me wonder."

"I'm real enough," Lee assured him, making her voice bright in an effort to counter the sudden thudding of her heart. "It's just that I'm lost."

He took a couple of swift strides across the room to switch off the stereo unit, which caused his bathrobe to separate and reveal an expanse of tanned, muscular leg to midthigh. Around thirty-five, he was tall and athletically built, with broad shoulders and slim hips. His face in profile showed a strong brow, a straight nose and firm, jutting chin. When he turned to look at her again and the light from one of the lamps shone full upon his features, Lee felt a curious shiver of excitement pass through her. In no way conventionally handsome, the man possessed a sensual vitality that zinged across the space between them. In a rushing chaos of unbidden thoughts, she imagined how it would feel to have those large, powerful hands caressing her skin; how delicious to run her own hands through the lush, tousled hair that was still damp from a shower. Would that firmly chiseled mouth become pliant and warm if pressed against her own mouth? She envisioned his eyes—deepset, smoky-brown eyes fringed with long dark lashes—regarding her with tenderness. Instead of which, she was being treated to a leisurely up-and-down appraisal, his gaze seeming to approve of her delicately molded features and long, slender legs, and clearly speculating about the feminine shape that lay beneath her belted raincoat.

"So you're lost," he said musingly. "Okay, I'll buy that. But I can't imagine where you were heading to have landed yourself here."

"I was on my way to Aberdyffryn, actually, but—"

"A strange route to choose."

"I didn't *choose* it," she returned, somewhat testily. "It's this wretched fog. I took a wrong fork somewhere, and by the time I realized my mistake I couldn't find anywhere to turn. So I kept going, hoping to get back to a proper road. Then mercifully I saw your light."

"So how would you like me to help you?" he inquired,

cinching the tie of his bathrobe a little tighter around his waist.

"Well . . . I just wondered what it's best to do. Keep on going, or—"

"If you kept on going," he interrupted again, "you'd end up axle deep in bog at the top of the mountain."

"Oh dear! Then perhaps you could help me get my car turned 'round . . . by reversing into your driveway, perhaps, with you making sure I don't back into a stone wall or something."

"No great problem there," he said. "But it's a minor miracle that you got this far in such foul weather. The way this fog's closing in, I wouldn't rate your chances of getting back to the road at better than fifty-fifty."

"But what else can I do?"

"There's only one answer to that question which makes any sense."

"Which is?"

"You'd better stay here overnight."

Lee's initial glow of thankfulness was instantly followed by a complex rush of emotions that she couldn't begin to untangle, except the embarrassment that was predominant. "I'd hate to put you to any trouble," she said awkwardly.

He studied her again, insolently at ease, seeming to be enjoying her discomfort. "No trouble. It'll be a pleasure."

She needed to get one or two quick answers. First off, she hazarded, "Your wife might not apply the same sort of logic to the situation."

"No wife." He grinned, seeing through her ploy.

"Are you . . . alone here?"

"Not now," he pointed out, his grin becoming broader. "Look, why don't you sit down and get yourself warm. What's your name, by the way?"

"Lee Jordan."

There was a short silence while she settled in one of the armchairs and appreciatively held out her small, slender-fingered hands to the blaze.

"*Mrs.* Lee Jordan," he said, and it wasn't a question. As she turned to look at him, he gestured to the plain gold band she wore. "I didn't need to be much of a Sherlock Holmes to know that you're married."

"Actually, my husband is dead," Lee told him. "He was killed in a car crash the winter before last." She saw no reason to add that her marriage had been virtually on the rocks for some while before that.

The man was silent for a token moment of sympathy. Then he became brisk and said, "It's settled, then. You're staying here. I'd better go and make myself decent. Then I'll fetch your things in from the car."

"It's very kind of you, Mr. . . . Er?"

"Call me Jake," he said, with a smile that seemed to melt her bones.

Jake. She liked the sound of it—a nice, clean-cut name that suited him. "Perhaps, Jake, you'll help me get the car safely off the road."

"No need. Nobody else is going to drive this way tonight, that's for certain. You can leave the car right where it is."

"If you're sure . . ."

"I'm sure." At the archway he turned back and added invitingly, "Help yourself to a drink."

Left alone, Lee stood up and slipped off her raincoat, then wandered around the room, possessed by a strange, restless, jittery feeling—which had to be attributed, she concluded, to the curious situation she was in. Her host seemed a pleasant man, an intelligent, interesting man, but those qualities couldn't account for the sensation that the blood in her veins had suddenly turned to champagne, seething and bubbling through her body until she felt deliciously lightheaded. She'd allowed no man to have this effect on her since those youthful days when she'd met and married Stephen. But in the months and years that had followed, her love had been dented time and again until her marriage had become an empty shell held together by merely practical considerations. The final pain had come after Stephen's death, when she learned at the inquest that the client killed with him in his car was a woman with whom he'd been having an affair for some time.

She paused at the drinks cabinet, considering what to choose. But alcohol, she decided, was the last thing she needed right now. Standing there, Lee raised her eyes to an oval-shaped mirror hanging on the wall, framed with carved oak leaves. In the muted radiance of soft lighting and the fire's dancing flames, the tan that remained from a long, hot summer made her skin glow with health. Her hair, which she wore twisted up into a sleek knot fixed with pins and a tortoiseshell comb, was a warm honey-blond that glinted with auburn highlights. She had neat, delicately shaped ears, and a small pointed chin that dimpled when she smiled. Her mouth was curved and generously full; her eyes, set candidly wide apart, were a clear, bright, sapphire blue.

A sound from behind made Lee swing around guiltily. "I was just . . . checking to see that I didn't look too much of a mess after my battle through the fog."

"You look fine," Jake assured her. Their eyes met and held, and Lee felt her heart skip a beat at the warm appreciation in his glance. With a slow smile, he added softly, "More than fine, Lee, you look good enough to eat."

Jake had pulled on a pair of fawn cord jeans and a white turtleneck, with his bare feet slipped into leather sandals. His hair, combed through but still not fully dry, gleamed dark against his suntanned skin. Lee dragged her gaze away and looked toward the fire. But the image of him, of his splendid physique, was still clearly imprinted on her retina. She had thought at first sight that his towering size was due to the low-ceilinged room, but a more careful assessment told her that he was well over six feet tall and broadly built—and all of it bone and muscle without an ounce of surplus flesh. The loose-fitting sweater did nothing to conceal the classical mold of his shoulders and chest, narrowing to a taut waist, and the lean-cut jeans hugged the shape of long, powerful thighs. Lee shivered, trying to crush down her disturbing thoughts.

"If you wouldn't mind fetching my luggage," she stammered, hardly able to get the words out for the dryness in her mouth. "You'll find it on the back seat. Oh, and I'd better give you my keys so you can lock the car."

Jake laughed. "Don't bother. Welsh mountain sheep are an honest lot." He disappeared through the front door and returned a couple of minutes later with her suitcase and carryall. "If you'd like to follow me, Lee, I'll show you where you can sleep."

He led the way up a narrow, boxed-in staircase that turned halfway. On the tiny square of landing were two doors. He threw open the one on the left, turning on a light as he went in, then bending to switch on an electric heater. It was a charming little room with a dormer window. Jake drew the chintz curtains, shutting out the view of fog, and turned on another light. There was a wide double bed with a beautifully patterned patchwork quilt, and underfoot was a thick shag-pile carpet in a soft shade of blue. Beneath the window stood an intricately carved wooden chest, and opposite the bed there was an oak tallboy on which rested various china ornaments. A silver-framed photograph looked suspiciously like Jake at about sixteen, wearing soccer gear.

"I haven't changed this room from the way my mother

had it before she died," he explained, a note of nostalgic fondness in his voice.

"This was your parents' home?"

"My grandparents', actually, and it was where my father was born. But he and my mother lived in Aber-dyffryn. They just used this cottage for weekends, as I do."

"I see. I imagine that it must be a charming place when the weather's fine."

Jake nodded. "Idyllic. But then, I guess I'm prejudiced. You'll see the view for yourself in the morning, if the fog has lifted. The bathroom's downstairs—the door facing you as you go down. I'll sort out some sheets for you, and then, when you're ready, we'll eat."

She laughed nervously. "I won't say no to some food. It's been a long time since I had anything. But you mustn't let me . . . I mean . . ."

"Don't worry," he assured her, "there's enough for us both."

He clattered downstairs and was back in a moment with the sheets. Alone, Lee made up the bed and unpacked what she needed before slipping down to wash. Upstairs again, she put on the pleated skirt and sweater she'd laid out already, then, on an impulse, she changed her mind, choosing a soft dress in a misty green angora wool, with a draping, crossover neckline. In her daily life she had enough of playing the career woman in a man's world, always as tough and forceful as her male counterparts. Tonight, just for once, she felt a stirring need to be feminine. It was a novel sensation, so novel that she wondered if she were being reckless. In the act of unpinning her hair, she paused. No, let that stay . . . as a sort of defense.

Descending the stairs, she found that the table places had been set, with a bowl of salad and a bottle of white wine misting coolly. Noises led her through to the kitchen. Jake was just taking a roast chicken out of the oven, and its delicious aroma filled the air.

"That looks scrumptious," she commented.

"It's a free-range bird. I get them from a farm in the valley." He put the roasting pan down, flicking the oven cloth over his shoulder as he turned to look at her. His eyes glowed in warm appreciation. "You've changed, I see."

She colored faintly. "I felt a bit travel stained, so I thought I'd better. You seem to be very well organized, Jake. Can I do anything to help?"

"You can lead the way with that dish of spuds."

At the table, he wielded the carving knife with expertise, deftly disjointing the chicken. Watching him, Lee remarked, "This is quite some meal. You seem to do yourself proud."

Jake quirked an eyebrow. "I wasn't planning to wolf down the whole chicken in one go."

"I should hope not." She laughed. "Am I depriving you of tomorrow's rations?"

"Put it this way, I shan't starve." He added another slice of white meat to Lee's plate, and asked, "Is that enough to be going on with?"

"Plenty, thanks."

She was ravenously hungry and the food tasted delicious. The wine was dry yet fruity, inducing a glowing warmth that radiated through her. "Where did you learn to produce meals like this?" she asked as she laid down her knife and fork.

Jake shrugged. "The theory that males are helpless in the kitchen is a myth fostered by women because they enjoy mothering us."

"Not *all* women," she corrected. "Personally, I've no time for a man who expects to be waited on hand and foot."

Jake leaned back in his chair and regarded her judicially, his eyes sweeping over her face and coming to rest on her mouth. "Tell me about yourself, Lee."

"Well . . . I'm an architect." There was a ring of pride in her voice.

He tilted his head. "That's unusual for a woman, isn't it?"

"Oh, the barriers are coming down fast in all the professions, Jake, so you men had better look out. There's nothing a woman can't do if she puts her mind to it."

"Don't be such an aggressive feminist," he tossed back. "So . . . what decided you to go in for architecture? Following in your father's footsteps, perhaps?"

"No, Dad was a lawyer. But I can thank my lucky stars that both he and my mother were progressive enough to believe that their daughter had as much right to a fulfilling career as a son would have had. Architecture was entirely my own choice. Right from the cradle I always played with building bricks rather than dolls." She took a sip from her wineglass, and asked, "What do you do, Jake?"

"Oh, a bit of this and a bit of that. Your husband . . . what line was he in?"

"He was an architect, too. We met during my last year at college, when he came to give a lecture on the preservation of old buildings, and later I joined his firm, Hammond and Jordan. Then, when Stephen was killed, I took over his partnership."

"You're doing well?"

"Not badly. Hammond and Jordan have quite a reputation for sensitive restoration and reconstruction work. That's why I've come to this part of the world. My partner and I have an appointment in Aberdyffryn tomorrow for preliminary discussions with a firm who want their factory enlarged."

Jake's eyes were questioning. "Why isn't your partner with you?"

"He's visiting his mother this weekend, and he'll be meeting me in Aberdyffryn first thing in the morning." Ashley had in fact wanted her to join him on the visit to his elderly mother, pointing out that it was en route, but she'd resisted the idea. She got along very well with her late husband's partner—now her own partner—but lately she'd been getting strong vibes that he wanted them to be partners in another, more binding way. It would have certain advantages, Lee acknowledged. She had a great respect for Ashley's ability as an architect, and as a man, he was pleasant company and moderately good-looking. If she ever did decide to marry again (which was still in doubt), could she bear to go through all the emotional turmoil of falling in love with someone only to be faced almost certainly—men being what they were—with the crushing blow of disillusionment? Better, surely, to marry for practical reasons the second time around, leaving love and its bitter aftermath to the starry-eyed idealists.

Jake refilled her wineglass. "Can I give you some more chicken, Lee?"

"No thanks, I've done very well."

"Some cheese, then?"

"No, really . . . I'm full."

"Still, you must find room to help me finish up these plums. They're really special." He selected a large ripe fruit from the bowl, leaned across and touched it to her lips. The dewy softness of its purple-bloomed skin, warm and cool at one and the same time, felt extraordinarily voluptuous and taking a bite was an almost involuntary act. Her teeth sank deeply into the meltingly ripe flesh, which set juices running down her chin. Laughing, Jake dabbed her dry with his napkin. The little episode had been no more than lightly playful, yet Lee found that her heart was thudding wildly from the sheer intimacy of it. She took a sip of wine to steady herself as she watched him relishing the remainder of the plum.

"Shall we have another?" he asked.

"No!" she jerked out. Then, needing a breathing space from the mesmerizing effect of this man's nearness, she stammered, "I . . . I'll just go and wash the dishes."

The smoky-brown eyes glinted with amusement. "I thought you said you weren't the mothering type."

"I'm not," she confirmed. "But I owe you that much, Jake, surely?"

"The coffee has been perking and it'll be ready by now. So let's just stack the dishes. Then we can sit by the fire and discuss what, if anything, you owe me."

It was a declaration of intent, but she didn't feel threatened. Okay, if Jake wanted to flirt, she'd play along. A man more eminently qualified to be flirted with she could scarcely imagine. She suddenly felt excited, tinglingly alive.

"Will you pour?" he said a minute later, placing the coffee tray on a low table before the sofa. "I'll find some mood music."

Lee filled the two cups while he sorted out a record and put it on the turntable. Soft piano music filled the room, a poetically wistful melody that tugged at her heartstrings.

"It's Debussy, isn't it?" she queried.

"I had a feeling this would be your sort of music." Jake turned off the one remaining light, which left just the warm glow of the fire. Then he came to sit beside her on the sofa. He took the coffee she offered him, added sugar and stirred it absently, his eyes on her face. The emotional charge between them was almost palpable. "I still don't quite believe that you're real, Lee," he said at last. "Appearing from nowhere like that, out of the fog, you might be just a delightful figment of my imagination."

"I'm flesh and blood, all right," she answered, a tense feeling in her chest.

Jake continued to study her through narrowed eyes.

Then, slowly, he reached out and touched the back of a finger to the softness of her cheek. "Yes," he murmured, deep in his throat. "I'm just about convinced that you are."

She cleared the thickness from her voice, and said chattily, "Do you come here to the cottage every weekend?"

"If I can. It's a bolthole, I suppose, when pressures begin to build up. I like the quiet, the solitude . . . a chance to think."

"So I ought to apologize for intruding on your solitude," she murmured.

"Your intrusion," he said softly, "is a case of virtue being rewarded. The hydrogenerator went kaput at midday and I had to spend the entire afternoon fixing it. This place is all-electric except for the fire."

"But no mains?"

"You've got to be joking. The nearest power cable is five miles away, over the mountain. Anyway," he continued, "as soon as I got the juice back on, I shoved the chicken in the oven, then showered off the grime. I came out here to change the record and found you . . . beautifully gift-wrapped."

"Gift-wrapped?" she asked, fully aware that she was playing his game.

"You looked very fetching in that belted raincoat and jeans, Lee. You look even more fetching in this dress. But why do you wear your hair in such a severe style? It would look fantastic floating loose about your shoulders. Now, let's see how it's fixed."

He leaned forward and his hands went around her neck, feeling for the pins.

"Hey!" Lee exclaimed, with a little thrill of pleasure at his touch. "What d'you think you're doing?"

Jake's face was only millimeters from hers, and she could feel his breath fanning her cheek. Tiny laugh lines radiated from the corners of his eyes as he looked at her questioningly. "You're not telling me that you never wear your hair down?"

"Well . . . sometimes."

"This is one of those times."

She was transfixed, as if held still by some superior force, while he deftly withdrew the tortoiseshell comb and the pins. Her silken hair tumbled down about her shoulders in a shimmering golden waterfall. Jake ran his fingers through it lingeringly, drawing it forward so that it framed her face in soft waves.

"You have such beautiful hair," he said huskily.

With a nervous flick of her head she tossed it back. "My mother told me to beware of flattery."

"Wise lady, your mother! A girl with your sensational looks must be constantly at risk from predatory males."

"No danger," she assured him, reaching for her almost empty coffee cup. But Jake checked her, taking her hand and stroking the palm erotically with his thumb. As a blissful sensation flooded through her, she went on nervously, falteringly, "I . . . I haven't reached the age of twenty-eight without building up an immunity to seductive tactics." But it was a patent lie and he would know it; she was betrayed by the leaping excitement which was making her whole body tremble.

Jake's dark eyes gleamed in the firelight as he smiled at her. Without speaking he lifted her hand and held her fingers against his mouth, brushing their tips with the point of his tongue. Lee's trembling intensified and her breath came jerkily, as if she were gasping for air. What was she letting herself in for? she wondered desperately. And then the defiant thought struck through . . . why not? She was a free agent, and there was nothing to be scared of—somehow she knew that, without a shadow of doubt. Wherever this situation led it would be *her* decision, *her* choice. Maybe it made sense to snatch the chances life threw her way, to be grateful for a brief, fleeting joy. Tomorrow morning when she left this cottage she would once again become Lee Jordan, architect, a competent professional woman making her mark in what was still largely a man's world. So just for tonight why not follow where her aroused emotions beckoned? Why not accept the offer of that almost forgotten ecstasy she had once upon a time shared with Stephen in the first heady days of their marriage, before things turned sour? Making love with Jake would be all of that and more, she knew instinctively, trembling at the touch of his searching fingers which had now invaded the opening at the buttoned cuff of her dress and were probing sensuously beyond. The slight rasp of his work-roughened male fingertips against the soft flesh of her forearm made Lee close her eyes as pulsing waves of heat washed through her body and she felt desire curling in her loins. She wanted Jake as she had never wanted any man since Stephen.

Oh God, what was she thinking? What had come over her that she allowed such a wanton thought even to enter her mind? She couldn't seriously be ready to jump into bed with a man she'd only just met this evening, no matter how attractive she found him.

But Jake was more than attractive, her thudding heart told her. The look in his eyes and the touch of his fingers had awakened needs and longings that she'd imagined were safely dormant, perhaps never to be aroused again. She had to fight him, fight herself, before this madness took full possession of her senses and she was swept away on a tidal wave of passion that drowned out the inner voice of common sense and discretion.

"Jake, please . . . this is crazy," she uttered in a choked voice, trying to release her hand from his grip.

"Not crazy," he denied. "It's indescribably wonderful.

You're so lovely, Lee. As lovely as any woman I've ever seen. Your eyes remind me of the sea on a bright summer day." He leaned forward and put his lips to the lobe of her ear. "And your skin is soft as thistledown . . . yet firm and warm and responsive."

She ought to be laughing at such wild, poetic extravagance of phrase—and she *would* laugh, she told herself, if any real man had said this to her. But Jake *wasn't* real, he couldn't be real. The smoldering virility that seemed to pulsate from him; the heady, musky male tang of him; the thrilling promise of those lips which had now left her earlobe and were tracing a pathway of tiny, nibbling kisses down the curving line of her jaw . . . all this was just a fantastic dream. She knew nothing whatever about him, and realized, as her scruples once again became submerged by the rising floodtide of passion, that she didn't *need* to know anything about him. This was no true-life relationship; they were like phantom ships that pass in the night, and that was how she wanted to keep it. Tonight would be so many hours stolen out of time, a little cameo memory to hold precious. She felt gloriously reckless, and when Jake's lips reached her mouth, she responded by sliding her hands around his neck and drawing him closer, letting herself melt against him.

"You're really something, Lee," he said breathlessly when at long last the kiss ended. "Fate sure was working overtime for me tonight, bringing down this fog and getting you lost in it."

"All for your special benefit?" she quipped with a shaky laugh. "What an outsized ego the man has."

"Are you claiming it's mere chance, you being here?"

"What else?"

He smiled deep into her eyes. "We won't argue the point. Either way, it's the same happy result. You're here, I'm here . . . we have the long night before us."

"My father," she said sententiously, "always used to say that one should never count one's chickens prematurely."

"You're full of the handed-down wisdom of parents, aren't you, Lee? *My* father taught me that one should never look a gift horse in the mouth."

She giggled. "You're calling me a horse, now?"

Jake tilted his head, considering. "A sleek, mettlesome racehorse, perhaps. Not a docile hack."

"I'm glad you understand that I'm not docile," she said.

"Docility is not a quality I admire in a woman."

"So what qualities do you admire?"

He leaned back against the sofa cushions and held up his left hand, the fingers outspread to count off his answers. "Beauty, of course, as long as intelligence goes with it. Spirit and courage and determination . . . that makes five already." He switched hands to continue. "Poise and serenity, gentleness, a sense of humor and a commitment to life. Shall I continue counting on my toes?"

"No, those will do to be going on with."

"You possess them all, Lee, and many more. The big one, the really important one, I've saved until last."

"The big one?"

He touched his forefinger to the tip of her nose. "You, my sweet girl, are very, very sexy."

"You're sure that's not just wishful thinking?" she said, ridiculously pleased. She realized how much she was enjoying the cut and thrust of this verbal fencing. These past two years, whenever a man had attempted to get fresh, she'd always slapped him down right at the start. But this time, with Jake, she wanted it to go on and on.

"Not wishful thinking," said Jake, shaking his head. "You're a very passionate woman, Lee. You may wear a prim mask for the world to see, but when you let your hair down—and I mean that literally as well as metaphorically—you're potential dynamite."

Lee swallowed, finding no words to answer. Her skin was tingling deliciously, and little eddies of excitement were pulsing through her veins.

Jake lifted a handful of her hair and nuzzled his face into it. "Mmm, you smell beautifully clean and fresh, like wildflowers and new-mown hay, plus all sorts of subtle oriental perfumes expressly designed to send a man's senses reeling." He touched his lips to each eye in turn. "There're roses from an English garden." He kissed her nose. "And lilies and gardenias, and honeysuckle on a warm summer evening." With the pointed tip of his tongue he traced the curving outline of her mouth. "And frankincense and myrrh, too, I shouldn't wonder."

Lee expressed a shuddering sigh. "Jake, I . . ."

He silenced her with a kiss, long and drowning, parting her lips to plunge in and curl his tongue around hers. One arm slid about her shoulders, drawing her closer against him, and with the fingertips of his other hand he traced sensuous little circles on her bare knee until she could have cried out with the joy and torment of it, wanting this bliss to last forever, yet desperately yearning for more. In a daze of delight she ran her hand across his chest, thrilling to the warm molded contours she could feel through the soft-coarse knit of his sweater. Reaching the ribbed neckband, she pulled it down so that she could slide in her hand and lay it against the smooth skin at the base of his throat, feeling the strong pulse that beat there.

The record he'd put on had long since ended. In the hushed silence a log shifted and the fire crackled with new life. It was part of the enchanted capsule enclosing the two of them; beyond was the great blanketing darkness of the fog that shrouded the deserted mountains.

A timeless age later Jake ended the kiss and they both

gasped for breath, smiling at one another in delighted wonderment.

"Oh Lee, Lee, you can't imagine what you're doing to me." Jake's voice came huskily from somewhere deep within him. "I can't remember when I've felt like this before. You're driving me wild."

She could feel the trembling of his fingers as he reached for the zipper at the back of her dress, easing it down in a soft whisper until it hung loosely around her shoulders. He remembered the buttoned cuffs and undid them, then swiftly pulled the dress away, lifting her slightly to draw it down over her hips and legs. Clad in just her transparent bra and panties, Lee felt a sudden rush of embarrassment. She turned her face away, but gently he drew her back and held her eyes in the grasp of his.

"No, Lee, you have nothing to be shy about. Your body is very beautiful, so why not enjoy having me look at you?"

For long, throbbing moments his gaze swept over her in lingering appreciation till she felt almost faint with the tension of it. She gave a convulsive shudder when Jake laid his two hands on the soft flesh of her stomach just above the top of her panties. Slowly, he slid them upward and outward over the silky skin, across her waist, curving over the swell of her breasts and smoothing along her shoulders to the slender column of her neck. Cupping her chin between his palms, he tenderly pressed a kiss to her mouth, then his lips followed a reversal of the trail his hands had taken, tracing a line of fire upon her skin. At her navel he halted and she felt the soft nudging of his tongue in exploration. Lee let out a shuddering moan and gripped his muscled shoulders with both hands, aroused to an almost frantic state of longing. But Jake slid away elusively to kiss the sensitive flesh of her thighs and legs, one hand reaching down to tug off the strappy high-heeled sandals so that he could caress her feet. Each bare toe came in for his ardent attention as he drew it into his mouth, sucking and biting with gentle savagery, lapping it with his tongue.

"Jake," she gasped, hardly able to bear the tormenting pleasure. "Oh, Jake . . ."

He moved then, coming up to find her lips once more in a kiss that left her drowning with delight. Nothing was real tonight; never in all her life had she experienced such an intensity of pleasure. Every nerve and cell in her body seemed more vibrantly sensitive than ever before.

Jake drew back from her a little and, smiling, his eyes seeming to devour her, he reached around to unhook the clasp of her bra and pull aside the gossamer fabric. At once her breasts sprang free into the eager cupping of his two hands, their dark red tips puckering to even greater rigidity under the exquisite torture of his circling thumbs. He bent and caught first one, then the other, between his lips, nipping and tugging until she was delirious with joy.

"You're magnificent, Lee," he breathed. "The way your flesh comes alive and burns under my hands. It's sensational."

Their eyes met and locked in a long glance that was so traumatic, so incredibly momentous, it felt to Lee as if all the breath had been suctioned from her body and she wondered if she would ever be able to breathe again. But she didn't care—she could happily die at this moment here with Jake.

His hands began to roam over her body once more, exploring, eliciting from the tender, secret places the most wonderfully thrilling sensations that built and built until she felt afloat on a cloud of pure happiness. He caressed her gently, stroking reverently, on and on in a ceaseless pursuit of her pleasure. Lee lost all account of time and place; the room and the flickering firelight receded into a soft aura of enveloping warmth, and it was just the two of them, a man and a woman in joyous abandonment of sensual delight. She clasped his head and drew him to her more closely, her fingers tangling into the crispness of his dark hair, while her body writhed in sinuous response to his questing hands and mouth.

Presently Jake pulled back from her and in one swift movement wrenched off his sweater. In the light from the fire's dancing flames the splendid proportions of his bronzed torso were revealed to Lee's awed gaze. As she involuntarily reached out to him, Jake caught her up in his arms, lifting her from the sofa and pulling her down to the fleecy softness of the sheepskin hearthrug. He held her closely in an iron grasp, his legs and arms wrapped around her, his mouth sealed to hers, his tongue thrusting in with erotic stabs in a kiss which made their earlier passion seem lukewarm.

"Sweet, lovely Lee," he murmured in a voice that was strained and cracked with desire. "You're so beautiful, I can hardly believe it. Oh God, how I want you!"

A shiver of delight rippled through her as he touched her again, his hands reverently shaping her breasts and caressing the soft skin of her stomach. But then, as he moved downward to slide his fingers beneath the elastic of her panties, it was as if something exploded in her brain. Suddenly the enormity of what was happening reached through to her benumbed wits. In a cold panic she pushed Jake's hands away and struggled to sit up.

"What's wrong, Lee?" he asked, sounding bewildered.

"I'm sorry," she stammered, glancing away in an agony of embarrassment. "I can't go through with it."

There was a long, long pause, then Jake said in a tight voice, "I thought this was what you wanted, Lee. I thought you wanted it as much as I did."

Lee shook her head wretchedly. "I'm sorry, Jake, truly I am." She felt the swift prickle of tears as she groped for words to explain. But how could she explain something that she didn't understand herself? Disjointed phrases jerked from her quivering lips. "I feel so dreadfully ashamed, having let you think that . . . I didn't intend to . . . to suddenly back off like this, but I can't help myself." She put her hands to her face, pressing them against her damp cheeks. "Oh God, I don't know what came over me tonight. I must have been mad, totally insane, to imagine that I could ever . . . I mean, you and I are total strangers. We didn't even know of one another's existence a few hours ago."

"And suppose we *had* known each other before, and then tonight had happened? Would that have made a difference to the outcome?"

"Perhaps," she murmured, after a moment's thought. "I . . . I just don't know. I'm not a promiscuous woman, Jake."

"I never imagined for a single instant that you were."

"This sort of behavior isn't like me at all," she rushed on. "I just don't begin to understand how I could act that way."

Jake's hand came up and lightly caressed her cheek. "Our meeting tonight was something unique and incredible, out of this world. From the first moment I set eyes on you I've wanted you like crazy. It seemed to me that you felt the same way about me."

She shook her head again, but not in denial. "I'm sorry," she repeated dully, still not able to meet his eyes. "It was all a horrible mistake. I shall never be able to forgive myself for—"

"You're being too hard on yourself," he interrupted. "Everybody makes mistakes sometimes. I'm not blaming you for backing off, Lee. It's just rather sad, because it could have been a very wonderful night for both of us."

She felt utterly drained and her whole body seemed cold as ice. It took a big effort to pull herself together. Bending to gather up her bra and dress, she turned her back to put them on and cover up her nakedness. She wanted to run out of the room and escape the scorching impact of Jake's gaze, but she steeled herself to act in a composed manner as she slipped on the bra and clipped it, then wriggled into the dress and manipulated the long zipper. Running fingers through her tousled hair, she flicked it back over her shoulders.

She was glad when she turned to face Jake to find that he too had dressed, dragging the white sweater over his head and covering that superbly muscled torso of his.

"I guess it would be best if I went straight up to bed," she muttered, slipping her feet into her sandals.

Jake gave a rueful smile. "Will you sleep tonight, Lee? I doubt if I will. A thin partition wall will separate us, that's all."

She couldn't repress the shiver that ran through her slender frame, and she knew that Jake must have noticed.

"Good-night," she said shakily, going to the door at the foot of the stairs.

"In case you should change your mind," he called after her softly, "there's nothing to stop your coming to my room. You'll find a warm bed and a very welcoming lover. Think about it, Lee."

2

As her car lurched and jolted laboriously down the narrow mountain byway, Lee marveled at the near miracle she had accomplished last night in driving up such a precarious track in thick, blanketing fog.

It was a morning of ineffable beauty, the air mild and sweet smelling, with only a slight mist remaining to haze the sun's golden brightness. The nearby mountains rose above her in vivid grandeur, but the far-off peaks that she glimpsed through the narrow pass at the valley's end were a delicate lilac blue, the sky above them streaked with soft apricot, as though from an artist's brush. On her right, a rushing, cascading stream foamed in its rocky bed. How easily she might have ended there upside-down, she thought with a sickening shudder.

Before joining the main road Lee stopped the car for a moment and turned in her seat to look back the way she had come. Her eyes could pick out the track, a tawny ribbon that snaked upward through the empty, boulder-

31

strewn landscape. And high, high up on the green slopes that were dotted with grazing sheep was the little cottage she had left, gleaming white in the sunshine, with not another dwelling anywhere in sight.

Up there, lost in a fogbound wilderness, she had spent a momentous night in a stranger's home. Incredibly, she had been on the verge of total intimacy with a man she'd never seen before and would almost certainly never see again. For this last thought she was overwhelmingly thankful. Yet, ridiculously, behind her relief was a wistful curl of regret.

Lee had descended from her bedroom in the morning, hollow-eyed and on edge, to find Jake in the living room. Just one glance at his tall, lithe figure, encased in hip-hugging blue jeans and a white T-shirt, had instantly reawakened all her feelings of longing, which had been even keener than her sense of shame and humiliation. Desperate to escape, she'd planned to leave the cottage without delay, but Jake had insisted that she stay for some breakfast.

"It's all ready," he pointed out. "Orange juice, cereal, toast and marmalade. Or I'll scramble you some eggs, if you like."

"Thanks all the same, but I don't normally bother with breakfast."

"Not even coffee?" he queried, with an ironic lift of the eyebrows. "You can't drive off like this on an empty stomach. Sit down, Lee, and I'll bring it in."

"Thanks," she said weakly, knowing how much she needed the lift of a cup of coffee.

As they had sat facing one another across the small table, making stilted conversation, Lee had constantly found Jake studying her face with an enigmatic expression in his smoky-brown eyes. Each time, she had looked away hastily, wretchedly aware that he must know she'd spent a tormented night. Had he guessed how sorely tempted she'd been to accept his invitation to his bed, despite everything? Sipping her coffee, she had fought against the memories of what had happened in that room last evening, flushing at how close she'd been to giving way to him. Held almost naked in his arms, she had responded with passion to his fevered kisses and caresses, only coming to her senses when they were almost past the point of no return. She had supposed, in the light of morning, that she ought to be thanking her lucky stars that Jake had taken her eleventh-hour decision so well, and not turned difficult. And throughout their morning coffee, he had given no sign of being resentful, but had appeared perfectly affable. Lee had even felt that he found cause for amusement in their situation. If so, he had a curiously warped sense of humor.

Lee had swallowed just one cup of coffee, and eaten barely half a slice of toast. Then, unable to stand it a moment longer, she stood up and announced in a crisp, practical voice, "I must be on my way."

"So soon?" Jake rose, too, his lips twitching in a faint smile. "What an eager beaver you are to get to work."

Damn him for laughing at her! Crossly, Lee strode to the front door, and only then remembered her suitcase and carry-all that she'd left at the foot of the stairs. Turning, she almost collided with Jake, who was bringing them across for her. She spun away from the physical contact as if stung, mortified to know that he was well aware of her reaction.

Outside, she made a dreadful hash of turning her car. When she was all set to drive off, Jake came to the lowered window and rested a hand on the ledge. Lee could see the tiny hairs at his wrist gleaming in the sunlight.

She wrenched her gaze away. "Well, good-bye. And thanks."

"Thanks for what, Lee?" he inquired with a slow grin.

"For . . . for giving me a meal and a bed."

"Oh that! It was nothing."

"I'd have been in real trouble if I hadn't spotted your cottage."

"And now you're out of trouble? Let's hope so, Lee."

Damn him again. He had known even then that at this moment she was longing for him to bend a few inches more and place his lips against hers, shuddering at the imagined bliss of it. She had clumsily snicked the gearshift into first. Jake had known as well as she did herself that it would be a long while before she ceased to tremble at the memory of his kisses and caresses. A long while before she ceased to fantasize about how it would have been the night before had she not called a halt when she did.

Now, as she drove on and took the road for Aberdyffryn, she still felt puzzled about Jake's attitude of the morning—more than just puzzled, she felt a bit piqued. If he weren't resentful about what had happened, she thought wistfully, he might have shown a little interest in the possibility of seeing her again. Suppose he *had* done so . . . suppose he'd suggested her having dinner with him at some restaurant in the vicinity . . . what then? But she didn't need to find an answer; the question was purely academic.

"Lee, where the devil have you been?"

As she pushed through the revolving doors of the Prince of Wales Hotel, where she'd made a reservation by phone a few days ago, Lee was startled to hear the familiar voice of her business partner. Breaking off his conversation with the desk clerk, he came striding toward her and took the bags from her hands.

"Hello, Ashley," she stammered, thrown at finding him here already. "I . . . I didn't expect you to have arrived yet."

"I decided to make an early start from Mother's," he explained. "I thought it would be a good idea for us to have a general look around the town before our appointment at Talbot Industries. But when I heard that you weren't here, Lee . . . that you hadn't occupied your room last night, I felt worried sick in case you'd had an accident."

Lee's brain whirled. She hadn't calculated that any need would arise for an explanation to Ashley about where she'd spent last night. Conscious of the warm color creeping to her cheeks, she made the best job of it she could. "The fog was so bad that I thought it would be wise to put up for the night en route."

"Oh, I see." Ashley was only partly mollified. "You might have thought to call and leave a message, in case I got here first."

"There . . . there wasn't a phone." True, so far as she knew. She hadn't seen any sign of a phone at Jake's cottage.

Ashley's sandy brows knitted in perplexity. "What kind of hotel was it, for heaven's sake, not to have a phone?"

"I didn't say it was a hotel. Actually . . . well, the place I stayed at was a private house. A cottage, in fact. They . . ." Yes, it definitely sounded better to use the plural pronoun. "They were very kind, giving me a meal and a bed."

Ashley glanced at his watch. "You'd better check in and find your room, Lee. With luck we'll still have just about time to do a quick tour of the town first. Please hurry—there's a love," he added with a winning smile.

As professional partners, Lee and Ashley often were away together on business trips—this was nothing new. Lee had a feeling, though, that this time it was Ashley's intention to push their relationship a stage further. Just a few months short of his fortieth birthday, Ashley Hammond was a good-looking man with a squarish open face, sandy hair and quiet gray eyes. He'd proved himself a stalwart friend and colleague, doing everything he could to help her through the trauma of Stephen's sudden death. Moreover, he had been ready and willing to let her step into her husband's shoes as an equal partner in the practice. There was no chauvinism about Ashley; man or woman, sheer ability was the only thing that counted with him in a professional relationship. But the two of them had always gotten along so well, rarely having more than the smallest difference of opinion, that it wasn't altogether surprising to Lee that Ashley should be considering her in a different role. Naturally he had allowed a decent lapse of time following her bereavement, but all the signs suggested that he'd decided it was the right moment to make a move.

Lee's feelings about Ashley were somewhat ambivalent. He was a really nice man, a kind and thoughtful man. A woman would have to look far and wide, she knew, to find a more considerate husband. On the few occasions that they'd spent an evening together—going to a play at the Bristol Old Vic or an orchestral concert at Colston Hall, preceded by dinner—his good-night kiss had been a pleasant experience. But pleasant was the operative word.

Ashley would be straightforward with her, Lee was sure about that, not deceitful and unfaithful as Stephen had been. When she'd first known him he had been living with a woman who was a successful interior designer. But they'd split up and she'd gone back to her husband, and since that time Ashley had formed one or two short-lived relationships. Lee suspected that having a sex life wasn't all that important to him. Pleasant, straightforward and faithful . . . admirable qualities, but would they be enough in a husband?

Returning downstairs from her room on the second floor with these thoughts revolving in her brain, Lee watched Ashley rise from a seat in the foyer where he'd been reading the morning paper. At once an image sprang to her mind of that other man, an image that was far more real and vivid than the one who actually stood before her. She caught her breath in sudden stabbing remembrance of Jake's arms around her, his hard body pressed to hers, his lips and tongue erotically plundering her mouth, his caressing hands sending ripples of joyous excitement through the whole of her being.

"Are you okay, Lee?" There was concern in Ashley's voice.

"Yes, I'm fine. Why do you ask?"

"You look a bit odd . . . sort of dazed."

"Rubbish." She laughed uneasily. "You're imagining things."

They used Lee's car, because it would be more convenient for negotiating the narrow streets than Ashley's large Jaguar. Aberdyffryn was a town with distinctive charm, proud of its long history. Only a sprinkling of its buildings were genuinely ancient, though; for the most part it dated from the affluent days of the early nineteenth century when sea bathing had first come into vogue. Driving along the curving esplanade, they admired the elegant hotels and columned residential terraces.

"It's easy to see why the local planning department has a reputation for being tough," Lee commented. "A town as attractive as this deserves to have vigilant watchdogs."

Ashley nodded. "And it's not only officialdom that's going to be hard to please. The management of Talbot Woodcraft is just as keen that nothing is done to the factory that might spoil the general ambience of Aberdyffryn. Which is precisely why Hammond and Jordan have been chosen for the job."

"We haven't been appointed yet," Lee reminded him.

"We will be, don't worry." Ashley always seemed

more blithely confident than she felt, a fact which bothered Lee from time to time. Perhaps, she would fret, she should try to cultivate this sort of masculine detachment, but she always found herself getting so involved in the projects she undertook.

The clock on the pierhead showed 10:50. Lee swung the car away from the seafront and drove to an area of the town where the houses were smaller and less elegant, interspersed with a certain amount of light industry. They soon located the Talbot Woodcraft factory, and she turned through an archway into a cobbled courtyard which was swept immaculately clean. The main building was a fine old Victorian structure in weathered mountain stone, originally designed as a woollen mill. A painted sign indicated the way to the offices on the second floor. In a small reception room they were greeted by a neatly dressed middle-aged woman with a plumpish figure and lively brown eyes, who stood up to greet them from behind a typewriter.

"Mr. Hammond and Mrs. Jordan, is it?" she queried in a soft lilting voice.

"That's right," agreed Ashley. "To see Mr. Talbot."

She smilingly gestured them to sit down, then announced their arrival on the intercom. "Mr. Talbot will not be keeping you waiting above a minute or two," she told them.

"This is my first visit to Aberdyffryn," Lee volunteered by way of making conversation. "It's a really beautiful town."

"There's nice it is to hear you say that." The woman beamed. "Our building extensions will be in good hands, I am thinking."

"We'll do our best for you," Ashley replied, adding with a chuckle, "and Hammond and Jordan's best, I might say, is very good indeed."

The phone buzzed, and the secretary rose to her feet.

"Come you with me now, please, and I'll take you through."

They crossed a small lobby and she knocked on the door opposite before throwing it wide open. "Mr. Hammond and Mrs. Jordan," she announced, and stood back for them to go past her.

Lee entered first, stepping briskly, then halted in her tracks so suddenly that Ashley bumped into her. Rising politely to his feet behind the large kneehole desk was the man from last night.

The few seconds it took Lee to get a grip on her scattered wits seemed like long hours of wretchedness. It was a swift surge of anger that saved her. How dare he make a fool of her like this? He'd known who she was—he must have known—from the moment she gave him her name last night. Yet he had cunningly concealed his own identity, fully confident that she wouldn't make the connection between "Jake" and the "J. Talbot" signature on the correspondence they had exchanged. No wonder, she thought bitterly, that he had seemed amused this morning at their situation. He must be tickled to death now, knowing how embarrassed and humiliated she was feeling at meeting him like this. But she was darned if she'd give him the satisfaction of betraying her feelings. She'd outsmart him by not displaying the smallest indication that they'd already met.

"Good morning, Mr. Talbot," she said in a clear voice as she took his outstretched hand. That was a testing moment, when his strong fingers enclosed hers in a firm grasp . . . strong, sensitive fingers that only hours ago had brought her such sensual joy. He gripped her hand fractionally longer than necessary, and his dark eyes met hers with a question. The only answer Lee gave him was a defiant glare, then she dragged her hand free.

Vaguely, as if from the end of a long tunnel, she heard

Jake and Ashley exchanging pleasantries. Somehow she found herself ensconced in a chair. The two men also sat down, and Jake Talbot leaned back in his swivel seat and regarded them benignly.

"I trust that neither of you had any problems getting here?" Behind the polite inquiry was a hint of mockery meant for Lee's ears alone.

"Mrs. Jordan had a spot of trouble," Ashley responded. "She set out yesterday and encountered bad fog. So bad that she had to cut her journey short and put up somewhere for the night."

"Really?" The dark eyebrows were hoisted in apparent surprise. "These freak fogs do happen now and then in the mountains. You had no difficulty yourself, Mr. Hammond?"

"No, the roads are quite clear today, fortunately. If Lee had left her traveling until this morning, too, she'd have saved herself a lot of discomfort and inconvenience."

Jake's smoke-brown eyes swiveled to her, derision flickering in their depths. "It sounds to me as if you had to rough it last night, Mrs. Jordan."

She succeeded in meeting his gaze without flinching. "The accommodation was adequate, thank you."

"I'm relieved to hear it. I'd hate to think that Welsh hospitality had been put to the test and found wanting."

Ashley threw her an odd look, sensing some kind of friction behind this apparently amiable exchange. There were several things to be made clear to Jake Talbot, she decided, but this was not the right moment. He was going to discover that her embarrassment was only fleeting . . . that she was perfectly capable of having a workable relationship with him, which from now on would be confined strictly to professional matters. To Lee's dismay the thought suddenly struck through that Jake might be under the illusion, with her right here in Aberdyffryn, that it would be easy enough for him to succeed where he'd failed last night. To disabuse him of any such idea, she turned to her partner and laid a friendly hand on his arm. For good measure she added a winsome smile.

"I'm sure, Ashley dear, that Mr. Talbot is a busy man. So shall we get down to business? Will you kick off?"

Ashley smiled back at her, looking pleased though somewhat surprised. Then he launched into an opening spiel about the way the firm of Hammond and Jordan worked, the sort of time scale involved in the project and the degree of cooperation they would need from Talbot Woodcraft in doing the preliminary survey. "We shall both of us be around for the first couple of days," he explained, "then I'll be returning to Bristol while Mrs. Jordan stays on here to work out a detailed scheme. Which is likely to take her a further ten days, we estimate. If all goes well, I plan to be back here at the end of next week so that we can present you with our outline proposals, Mr. Talbot. We should then be able to give you enough data concerning the finished appearance of the extensions to your factory, and the probable cost, to enable you to judge whether or not to proceed any further."

Jake nodded. "That sounds reasonable to me."

"Naturally," Ashley continued, "we expect you to explain the position fully to your employees. If they were to get the idea that we represented some kind of vague threat to their jobs, they might prove uncooperative when Mrs. Jordan goes around asking questions."

Jake's smile embraced them both, but lingered a second longer on Lee. "I can't imagine anyone being uncooperative with Mrs. Jordan," he remarked. "However, I take your point, Mr. Hammond, and I'll insure that the staff here are put fully in the picture."

They talked some more, then Jake sent for three of his senior executives. "Mr. Emlyn Davis," he introduced, "who is our chief production controller. Mr. Dylan Lambert, our works manager. And this is Mr. Huw Clarke, our financial wizard." He grinned. "All your estimates will have to get past Huw's eagle eye."

They all chatted for a while, then Lee and Ashley were led off by Dylan Lambert on a tour of inspection. He was a stocky, cheerful man with wiry gray hair. It soon emerged that he was extremely proud of the factory under his control. Lee noted that though it was well equipped with modern woodworking machinery, there was no attempt at automation.

"The boss insists, and I wholeheartedly agree with him, that making quality furniture is a job for craftsmen, not for soulless robots." Dylan ran a work-toughened hand across the newly planed top of a dining table, and added with a little smile, "Wood is a very special raw material, Mrs. Jordan. Even though a tree has been cut down and sawed up, the wood is still alive and breathing. It still has a heart and a soul. It's something you can love passionately, which most of us who work here do."

And that no doubt included the boss, Lee reflected. Was this Jake's one and only real love? I pity the woman he eventually marries, she thought with an involuntary shiver. His wife would share his home and bear his children, but would she ever get through to the essential Jake Talbot? Wistfully, Lee let her fingers glide around the satin-smooth back of a fine windsor chair made from English yew. There was a marvelous, voluptuous feel to the wood, a subtle combination of hardness and softness with a vibrant inner warmth. Like, she mused dreamily before she could censor out the thought, Jake's superbly muscled, virile body. . . .

"To see the finishing shop," Dylan continued, "I'm afraid that we have to cross the street. That's our main problem here: being so scattered. The firm has expanded so fast these past few years that we've had to take over whatever premises we could lay our hands on, however unsuitable. But you'll get that all sorted out for us, thank heaven. I can't wait for the day when we have every production department under one roof."

"I gather," said Lee, pulling her wits together, "that Mr. Talbot's father started the business here."

"You could almost say, Mrs. Jordan, that it was his grandda's doing. Joshua Talbot lived in a cottage up in the mountains, and he used to provide various services like sheep dipping and shearing for local farmers. But his hobby was woodwork, and whatever he made in his spare time always found a ready buyer. His son, that's Jake's da, inherited the old man's skill and he it was who started Talbot Woodcraft—just in a small way of business. Then Jake came along, and besides being a fine craftsman like his father and grandfather, he has a good head for business. Since he took over from his da it has really thrived."

"So there's more to Jake Talbot than the efficient factory owner," Ashley remarked. "I had a feeling, didn't you, Lee, that he's a man with hidden depths."

Lee, aware of her heightened color, turned away quickly and paid close attention to a small gateleg table. Dylan went on cheerfully, "I will tell you this, Mr. Hammond, there's not a single job in the factory that Jake couldn't do every bit as well as the operatives here. Of course, he doesn't have the time nowadays for anything but the managing. But he's kept on that little cottage I mentioned . . . it's his retreat, where he can unwind on weekends and so on. His grandda's workshop is still there, with all the old tools and everything lovingly preserved. And used, I might add . . . Jake's always working with the wood in one way or another, designing new lines for us to make here." Dylan smiled at them both. "You ought to get Jake to invite you up there sometime. You'd find it interesting."

"Good idea!" said Ashley approvingly, and glanced at

Lee. "You might fix a visit next Saturday or Sunday, if he's planning to be there."

Nothing on earth would persuade her to set foot inside that mountain cottage again, she thought with a shiver. But there was no way she could explain that to Ashley. "I doubt if I'll have the time," she murmured lamely.

"Oh, surely! Anyway, you'll need a break by then. I only wish I could return here for the weekend, but I'm afraid there's no chance of that, Lee. I'm behind schedule on that branch library at Landhurst."

Dylan led them through a workshop where four cheerfully chitchatting women were deftly weaving rush seats onto the frames of ladderback dining chairs . . . just like the ones Lee had seen at the cottage. Next door was the woodyard, then they walked farther along the street to a separate building that housed the packing shop. Adjoining this was a quiet little pub called the Mermaid, and Dylan suggested they drop in for a drink. They sat in the snug bar, where engravings on the walls depicted Aberdyffryn in the days when it had been just a small fishing village. The aroma of the landlady's homemade shepherd's pie was so appetizing that they decided to stay and have lunch there before continuing the tour of Talbot Woodcraft.

By six o'clock Lee and Ashley were back at their hotel, after a busy afternoon during which they'd also called at the local town hall to talk to Aberdyffryn's planning department officials.

"What I need more than anything is a long soak in a hot bath," Lee said with a sigh. "I'll see you later on, okay? Say seven-thirty?"

Ashley caught and held her hand for a moment as they stood at the head of the stairs before separating to go to their rooms. "I'm really looking forward to our evening, Lee," he said, smiling into her eyes. "You and I seem to get so little chance for being together, just the two of us."

Lee pulled her hand away—gently, because she didn't want to hurt his feelings—but she was anxious not to encourage him. Once in the sanctuary of her room, though, she had no thoughts to spare for Ashley. She had been waiting all day, with a growing feeling of desperation, for a chance to be alone and try to slow down the spinning chaos in her mind.

It had been one thing to instruct herself firmly that she would demonstrate to all concerned her total dedication to her job . . . one thing to vow that she would remain entirely unflustered by the need to have frequent meetings with Jake Talbot. But carrying out her resolve was something else altogether. Maybe, she thought frantically, she could get Ashley to take over her role here. Let him stay on in Aberdyffryn and handle the feasibility study at Talbot Woodcraft. But that was impossible, she knew. Aside from the fact that their respective schedules had been arranged for her to be free of other commitments for the ensuing two weeks, there was no doubt that this particular job was very much in *her* area of the partnership. While Ashley concentrated more on new structures, her own specialty was the conversion and extension of existing buildings. No, she thought gloomily, either she had to find a good reason for Hammond and Jordan abandoning the whole project, or she had to go through with it despite Jake's disturbing sensual magnetism.

After a long, relaxing bath to which she'd added lashings of jasmine essence, she toweled herself dry and got dressed for the evening, putting on a swirling taffeta skirt in royal blue, teamed with a navy broderie anglaise blouse. Then she sat at the dressing table to do her hair and make up her face. She still couldn't shake Jake Talbot out of her thoughts. Staring at her reflection in the three-way mirror, she asked herself why she should let last night take on such a major significance, when to Jake it was obviously no more than a hoped-for one-night stand which had ended disappointingly. Why did she feel this overwhelming sense of shame and guilt at what had happened? Okay, so yesterday evening Jake Talbot had come close to being her lover. But he hadn't succeeded, and today and from now on he was just a client.

The phone by the bed gave a discreet buzz, and Lee stood up and went to answer it.

"Mrs. Jordan? Desk here. Mr. Talbot is asking if he can see you."

"Mr. . . . Mr. Talbot?" she repeated stupidly.

"Mr. Jake Talbot. He says he'll be in the cocktail lounge if you would be good enough to come down."

"Tell him . . ." Tell him to go to hell, was on the tip of her tongue. But then defiance took over. Much better to face the man and spell out plainly just what she thought of his outrageous behavior. If he took the huff and wanted to back out of the agreement with Hammond and Jordan . . . okay. She'd have to fudge some kind of explanation for Ashley. "Tell Mr. Talbot that I'll be down in about ten minutes," she finished.

She rechecked her hair and makeup . . . not for his benefit, she told herself, but for the sake of her own self-confidence. Then, on legs that felt boneless, she made her way downstairs. In this Victorian-era hotel the cocktail lounge was a somewhat grand room leading off the foyer through an archway draped with crimson-velvet swags. At this early hour of the evening it was uncrowded. Jake's tall commanding figure rose from a table near the window and came toward her. There was, she noted with satisfaction, a look of wariness in his smoky-brown eyes, as if he were uncertain of his reception—as well he might be!

"Hi, Lee," he greeted her in a low, intimate voice, his glance sweeping over her slender shape with obvious approval. "I thought that a few words on our own would be a good idea."

"Whatever made you think that?" she asked sarcastically.

He ushered her to the table, his hand hovering just an inch or two from her elbow—a fact of which Lee was electrically aware. She sat down rather primly while Jake hunched himself comfortably into the adjoining chair.

"I got the feeling at my office this morning that you were mad at me."

"What else did you expect, for heaven's sake?"

"That you'd be pleased to see me again. Instead of which you seemed dead anxious that Ashley Hammond didn't catch on to the fact that we'd met before."

"Well, naturally . . ."

"You gave me no clue last night that you and your partner had something going between you."

"We haven't," she stated.

"Really? So why did I get the opposite impression when I saw you together?"

"You must have got your wires . . ." Lee braked to a stop. She had deliberately tried to give Jake the idea that she and Ashley were more than just business partners, so wasn't it sensible to stick to that line? She started again with cool dignity, "Whatever there may or may not be between Ashley Hammond and myself, I can't see that it's the slightest concern of yours."

Jake regarded her through narrowed lids. "It could make things . . . awkward for you, if anything were to come out about last night."

She felt herself go pale. "Are you threatening me?"

"Just pointing out the tricky situation you've landed yourself in. Lucky for you, though, I'm no blabbermouth. But you didn't know that when you threw yourself into the arms of a total stranger."

"That's a rotten thing to say."

"Meaning that I had to do all the pursuing? Come off it, Lee, you were just as ready and eager as I was until you suddenly went cold on me. You tried to have me believe that you'd lost your courage merely because you and I were total strangers. But I can see now that you were hit by an attack of guilt for cheating on Hammond."

"That's total garbage," she said, flaring indignantly. "It was just the way I told you. Nothing whatever to do with my relationship with Ashley."

"Okay, if you say so. It's your conscience that's on the line, not mine." He treated her to a slow, sensuous smile. "If it's true, what you claim, then we're back to the fact that what happened last night . . . or rather, what *didn't* happen, was very sad. You're a warm-blooded, gloriously passionate woman, Lee, with a body that is beautifully ripe for loving. I'll tell you this, sweetheart . . . the way you appeared like that out of the fog, looking so utterly desirable, almost made me believe in miracles. When something clicks like that between a man and a woman, when their chemistry is so fizzingly right, it's crazy not to grab the chance. Life doesn't hand out so many bonuses that we can afford to pass one up."

She regarded him with loathing. "And that's the Jake Talbot philosophy, is it?"

"D'you know of a better one?" he countered.

The elderly waiter came for their order. Lee asked for a straight vermouth on the rocks, and Jake a scotch and soda. When the man had pottered off, Jake said persuasively, "Lee, there's no need for you and me to be at daggers' point."

She nodded curtly. "I agree. All I want is a simple, straightforward business relationship with you. We've said all that's necessary about last night and cleared the air, so let's leave it there. We'll be client and architect, just that, and wipe the rest from our minds."

"Easier said than done. I shan't forget last night in a hurry, Lee, and I don't think you will, either. What's more, I don't want to forget it. Even though last night didn't quite live up to its promise, it was still a very wonderful evening."

"So wonderful," she said sarcastically, "that you were perfectly ready to let me drive off this morning without expressing the slightest wish to see me again."

Jake seized on her lack of logic. "But I knew that I'd be seeing you again . . . in my office."

"I didn't know that, though!" Lee's face flooded scarlet as she realized she'd betrayed her disappointment that he hadn't attempted to date her. The drinks arrived at that moment and she sipped hers nervously, wondering how to backtrack. An interruption saved her the need to say anything.

"Hello there, Lee. I've been wondering where you'd gone to." It was Ashley, coming through the archway into the cocktail lounge. "Oh, and Mr. Talbot," he added in surprise.

"I . . . I was ready," she stammered, "so I came down, and . . . and . . ."

"We bumped into one another," Jake finished for her. "I drop in here for a drink now and again, after a long day at the factory. What's your poison, Mr. Hammond?"

"I'll have a dry martini, please."

Jake went to the bar to fetch it himself this time, which gave Ashley a chance to say reproachfully, "Lee, why didn't you let me know you were coming down early? I'd have joined you."

"I'm sorry. I . . . I didn't think."

"Oh well, no harm done. Besides, it's always useful to socialize with a client." When Jake rejoined them, Ashley said with an inviting smile, "Lee and I have been wondering, Mr. Talbot, if you'd care to join us for dinner."

"Oh no!" Lee's involuntary protest sounded appallingly rude, but Jake just smiled and said easily, "I only wish I could, Mr. Hammond. But I'm afraid I have a prior engagement. Some other time, perhaps, when you return to Aberdyffryn to present your report. But then, I insist, the dinner must be on me."

Jake stayed chatting for ten minutes or so, then glanced at his watch and at once rose to his feet. "If you'll excuse me, I must be off now."

Reluctantly taking the hand he held out, Lee felt a shiver run through her at the remembered delight of that same hand passing caressingly over her naked flesh. With whom, she wondered with a poignant twist of her heartstrings, was the appointment he was so anxious not to be late for?

"Nice chap," Ashley commented as they watched him walk away with long, fluid strides. "I think we'll find him an agreeable client to work with." He smiled at her, ruefully amused, and laid a hand on her forearm. "I must say it was a relief that he took no offense when you made it so clear that you didn't want him to dine with us. I know exactly how you felt, my dear. I didn't want him to dine with us either. But there are times, alas, when we have to go through the motions of courtesy with clients, however much it's against our own inclinations."

Lee bit her lip, wishing she could edge away from the possessive touch of Ashley's hand without appearing too obvious. "I have a feeling that politeness would be wasted on a man like Jake Talbot."

"What makes you say that?" Ashley asked, surprised. "He's perhaps a little unpolished, but that's often the way with self-made men."

"Do you trust him, though?"

"That's not really important, is it? I mean, the financial side of things will be taken care of by our respective lawyers. Whether he decides to use our preliminary proposals or not, he'll still have to pay us for the work we've done. So what are you worried about?"

"Oh . . . nothing," Lee responded with a bright, false smile. "You're absolutely right, Ashley, and from now on I shan't give Jake Talbot another thought, except as a client."

Empty words, even as she said them.

The dining room at the Prince of Wales Hotel was ornately splendid, glittering with gilded mirrors and crystal chandeliers. Ashley studied the elaborate menu approvingly. He enjoyed good food, with the result that his midriff was showing the first warning signs. Lee found herself mentally comparing his physique with the sleek muscularity of Jake, whose stomach was flat and rock hard.

"What do you think, Lee?"

"Think? What about?"

"What to eat, of course. I suggest you try some Wye salmon to start with, followed by crown of Welsh lamb."

"Sounds delicious. But Ashley . . . I'm not terribly hungry."

"Nonsense. You've had a hard day's slog with only a snack in that pub at lunchtime. Now, about the wine . . . I wonder if they have a decent Moselle?"

It was a difficult evening. She had been right in thinking that Ashley saw this trip to Wales as a chance to move their relationship onto a different level.

"Back in Bristol," he mused, "the fact that we're business partners means that the job seems to intrude on every aspect of our lives. But there's more of a vacation atmosphere here and—"

"Some vacation," she cut in nervously. "I've got a fortnight of solid grind ahead of me, don't forget."

"Yes, but you know what I mean." Ashley's smile was warm and tender. "We don't need to feel that every move we make is being observed by people who know the two of us. We can be more relaxed, act more naturally."

"I suppose so," Lee said in a neutral voice. She wasn't going to give him any encouragement, but even so, she was afraid that Ashley wouldn't easily be deterred. He had never been a man to act impulsively; he gave careful thought to each and every situation. She guessed that having taken a decision about this trip, he intended to persevere even though the going proved difficult.

All through dinner she fended him off tactfully, smilingly, doing her best to keep the conversation lighthearted but impersonal. Afterwards, they sat in the lounge over coffee, with which Ashley sipped a brandy liqueur. Lee mentioned casually that she had a slight headache—true enough, in fact, from the strain and tension of the day. Her motive was to pave the way to her going up early to her room and gaining some longed-for solitude.

"A little stroll along the seafront is what you need," Ashley suggested sympathetically. "It's a lovely moonlit evening, and the fresh air will clear your head."

To refuse would have been churlish, and she didn't want to hurt his feelings. "I'll just slip upstairs for a shawl to throw around my shoulders," she said.

With the summer season over, there were few other strollers. The moon hung in a soft, ink-blue sky, seeming so near that you could almost touch it with outstretched fingers. The sea lapped the sandy beach gently in its eternal rhythm, and there was an elusive sound of music floating on the silk-soft air.

Ashley drew her hand through his arm and held it there with a gentle, friendly pressure. They paced along together in silence, right to the farthest breakwater where the esplanade buildings finished and there was a recreation ground with tennis courts and bowling greens, strung with colored fairy lights. Ashley halted, and as Lee wheeled for the walk back, she found herself facing him, almost touching. She felt his hands on her shoulders, gripping her gently.

"How's the head, darling?" he asked softly.

Darling! He had never called her that before. Should she correct him, make it clear that she didn't welcome the endearment from him? Best, she thought, to let it pass as if unnoticed.

"Not so bad," she replied with a shrug.

"I'm glad." He hesitated, then raised a tentative hand and touched the silken softness of her hair. "You're very beautiful, you know, besides being so intelligent and capable. There's no woman I admire more than I admire you."

She was silent, still wondering how best to handle this delicate situation now that it had come. She simply mustn't let things get out of hand, yet to repulse Ashley's advances too definitely would be cruel. Besides, could she yet be a hundred percent positive of her own feelings about him? If Ashley were now ready to settle down and marry, he would undoubtedly make a far more reliable husband than the type of man she could imagine falling head over heels in love with . . . like Stephen. Like . . . she tried to crush down the name and failed. Like Jake Talbot.

Her silent uncertainty seemed to have given Ashley a misleading impression. The next moment she found herself enfolded in his arms, his lips pressed to her hair. "I'm getting to be very fond of you, my dear . . . very fond indeed."

"Ashley, I . . . I'm not sure that—"

He stifled any protest she might have made by kissing her full on the lips. While Lee was analyzing her reaction to the kiss, she heard and saw a car approaching along the near-deserted esplanade . . . a long, low, white car. She found herself looking over Ashley's shoulder straight

53

into the eyes of the driver, dark eyes which glinted in the moonlight. The car had gone past before she could read Jake's expression, or do more than register the fact that there was a woman in the seat beside him. Who was she? Lee wondered, a chill striking her heart.

Firmly breaking away from Ashley, she murmured, "I'm sorry, but my headache seems to be getting worse. I'd like to go back to the hotel, if you don't mind. An early night is what I need."

3

Lee was soon well dug into the job at Talbot Woodcraft. She had established a good working relationship with the staff and found that her numerous questions were readily answered. Inevitably, the men sometimes whistled after her and made mildly suggestive remarks, but she parried them with well-practiced backtalk.

Ashley had started home for Bristol late on Tuesday afternoon without having found another opportunity to get intimate, for which Lee was thankful.

"I've been thinking," he said as they parted, "I'm going to try and work it so that I can come back and spend the weekend here. For one thing, it would be a good idea to follow up that suggestion of Dylan Lambert's and get Jake Talbot to invite us to his place in the mountains."

"No!" Lee said emphatically, dismayed at the thought of returning to Jake's cottage in Ashley's company.

"No?" He frowned. "But you know how useful it can

be to see clients in their domestic surroundings, and get an idea of what makes them tick."

"I . . . I meant no about you coming for the weekend," she faltered. "You've got more work on hand than you can comfortably manage as it is, with that branch library contract. And as for me, I'll really have to knuckle down if I'm to get this preliminary report done in proper detail. So I should forget about the weekend, Ashley."

He nodded, smiling his regret. "You're right, of course. But don't push yourself *too* hard on the paperwork, Lee darling, and if the chance comes up, do try to fit in a visit to that cottage of Talbot's."

No way will I do that, she thought fiercely as she waved Ashley off.

Jake Talbot, it had emerged from answers to her casual inquiries, was away for a few days at an exporters' conference in Birmingham. But on Friday morning when she drove into the firm's courtyard and parked her car, she saw Jake's big white Mercedes standing in the space reserved for the boss of the firm. Later, when she was busy taking measurements in the turning shop, where blocks of wood were shaped on lathes for the legs of Jacobean-style tables and chairs, she received a summons to Jake's office. Wondering, uncertain and nervous, she made her way across the street and up the stairs of the main building.

Seeing Jake again after a lapse of several days caused her heart to throb painfully. He struck her as even more devastatingly attractive than she had remembered. His jacket and tie had been thrown aside on a chair, and his textured cream shirt was open at the neck, revealing the bronzed skin of his throat where she had laid her hand that night, feeling the strong pulse that beat there.

"How are things going, Lee?" he asked with a warm, easy smile.

"Oh . . . fine."

"You're being given all the cooperation you need?"

"Yes, thanks. Everyone is being most helpful."

"Good." He paused, his smoky-brown eyes regarding her intently. "Your evenings—since Monday, that is— must have been rather lonely, with you stuck here in a holiday resort town at the tail end of the season. There's not an awful lot going on in Aberdyffryn at this time of year. At least, not for the strangers in town."

"I've been far too busy to feel lonely," Lee told him. She marveled that her voice could sound so calm and businesslike while her whole body was trembling from the effect of Jake's blood-stirring magnetism.

"You mustn't overdo things and knock yourself out. I'd hate to have that on my conscience." Behind his blandly pleasant expression, was he laughing at her? she wondered dismally. "I was thinking, Lee, that you and I might get together over the weekend."

She stared at him, stunned. Did Jake really imagine that she would happily return to his mountain cottage for a replay of Sunday night's encounter between them— this time with a different ending? His arrogance was beyond belief.

"No, thank you," she returned stiffly.

"Why not?" He came around the desk and stood close to her, his height and breadth and virile presence dominating her, intoxicating her. "Lee, you can't still be mad at me for not admitting who I was on Sunday night."

"Too darned right I'm still mad at you. You should have said who you were the moment I told you my name."

"And then what?" he inquired with a long, searching look. "Would our relationship have progressed in the same interesting way?"

Lee was silent, having no answer to give him. She fought against the hot wave of color she could feel rushing to her face.

A slow smile curved Jake's lips. "Try to see things from my point of view. I came through from the bathroom to find you standing there in my living room . . . a beautiful apparition from out of the fog. Then I learned to my astonishment that you were Lee Jordan, one of the architects I'd be meeting the very next day. To have revealed my identity then would have put a real damper on the incredible flare-up of magnetism between us." His smoky-brown eyes seemed to be carving through to her soul. "It was fantastic, Lee, fantastic for both of us. You can't pretend otherwise. Even though it didn't quite follow through as it should have done, that night was very special."

Lee couldn't hold his challenging gaze. Jake was right. She would only make a fool of herself trying to deny that she had reached a delirious level of sensual excitement with him that had promised supreme fulfillment. The fact that those blissful moments in Jake's arms had all been due to a gross deception on his part didn't alter the simple, basic truth.

"At least," she murmured huskily, "you might have had the decency to tell me in the morning, to put me on my guard."

"You didn't give me much chance to tell you anything, if you remember. You were so uptight and you couldn't get away from me fast enough. But I imagined that when you'd had some time to think things over and to realize the heaven-sent chance you'd thrown away the previous night, you'd be pleased to discover that you'd be seeing more of me. I visualized you laughingly telling your partner that you and I had met before—without of course going into details. I hadn't the least idea, don't forget, that you and he were more than just partners in a professional way."

"We're not," she flashed back.

Jake allowed his eyes to widen in an expression of

58

surprise. "You nearly got me to believe you, Lee, when you insisted that to me before. Then, later that same evening, I witnessed a romantic little scene in the moonlight."

"It wasn't romantic," she protested. "Just . . . just a good-night kiss."

"At the far end of the esplanade? When you were both staying at the same hotel?"

Lee felt cornered. But then, she thought defiantly, why the hell should she explain or excuse herself to Jake? "Listen," she snapped, "you can believe whatever you like about me and Ashley."

"I don't give a damn about you and Ashley. It's you and Jake Talbot that concern me, Lee. Now, about the weekend . . ."

"Some hope!" she retorted crisply. "I'm not setting foot in your cottage again."

"Pity," he said mildly. "But that isn't what I'm suggesting. I have a sailboat, and I thought we could have a trip along the coast tomorrow."

Jake had caught her off guard. But it made no difference. She wasn't about to spend any more time alone with him . . . *anywhere*. As she started to spell this out, Jake closed the gap between them and pulled her into his arms. His kiss, hard on her lips, sent darts of quivering excitement, of vulnerable weakness, shooting through her limbs. But she rallied her determination and thrust back from him.

"Don't do that," she ordered.

"Why not?" he said, his voice grating harshly, the gaze of his stormy-dark eyes seizing and holding hers. "Are you afraid of letting me kiss you, Lee?"

"Why should I be afraid? I just don't want you to, that's all."

"Then why are you trembling?"

"If I'm trembling," she said recklessly, "it's from anger.

Get this straight, Jake. Just because you'll be paying a high fee for my professional advice, you don't get a few favors thrown in as a bonus. If you thought so, forget it."

"Who's talking about favors?" he ground out. "The feeling between us Sunday night was mutual, shared, equal. Something unique and wonderful."

Catching her breath, Lee said in a whispered protest, "Let's leave it at that then, Jake. It happened. It's over."

"Do you really think it's over?" His eyes raked her face with the savage question. "Holding you like this I can feel your pulses racing. My own heart is beating enough to choke me. *Over*, Lee? What there is between us is only just beginning, and you know it."

Inexorably, he drew her close again, enfolding her with his arms. This time his kiss was not sudden and savage; this time his lips came slowly to meet hers, and Lee waited like someone in a trance. She gasped at the first soft contact, moaned as his warm mouth enclosed hers and his marauding tongue thrust between her lips in thrilling, erotic plunder. Her senses swirling, she let herself melt against him, her hands spreading out across the solid strength of Jake's back and feeling the sensual heat of him through the thin fabric of his shirt. Weak with delight, she clawed at the muscled contours of his shoulders, then tugged at his hair and plunged her fingers into its crisp, curly thickness. And all the while Jake's hands roamed over her body, claiming total freedom, sliding down her back and over her waist to clench into the yielding flesh of her buttocks, then moving around the smooth curve of thigh and hip and sweeping upward again. His fingers slid beneath her sweater and, through the filmy barrier of her bra, he held and fondled her breasts, teasing the already tingling nipples to peaks of almost unbearable yearning. His body, pressed against hers, was taut and tense, pulsing with the throb of his desire.

"Lee," he said, passion thickening his voice to a low, throaty growl. "I want you. Oh God, how I want you! And you want me too, don't you? Admit it."

"Yes," she sobbed. "Yes, Jake, I want you!"

She rejoiced in the fact that he desired her so intensely, found it almost unbelievably wonderful to have met a man who stirred her emotions to such a frenzy of wanting. If only it were possible, she would willingly let him take possession of her then and there in his office, without a moment's delay.

Jake covered her face with tiny kisses that were tender yet ardent, flooding her through with warm joy and making her veins thrum. "I wish that we could be together this evening, sweetheart, but I have an appointment over in Shrewsbury that I can't cancel. Tomorrow, we'll have all day long to ourselves." The phone on his desk rang, but Jake took no notice. "Think of it, you and me alone on the wide blue sea."

"Shouldn't you answer that?" Lee said uneasily, trying to draw herself out of his arms. But he wouldn't let her go.

"In a minute. I want to fix things about when and where to meet you. How about ten o'clock at your hotel . . . okay? I'll bring along a picnic hamper."

"But, Jake . . ."

"Wear casual gear," he instructed. "And don't forget a parka or something. It can get chilly on the open water when the wind blows up." Lee hesitated, debating with herself, and he added insistently, "Go on, say yes."

"Yes, Jake." It was inevitable, so why attempt to fight it?

"Right." He nodded in satisfaction, and grinned. "Better keep out of my way today or don't blame me for the consequences. It's going to be hard enough as it is to contain my impatience until tomorrow." On legs that trembled Lee crossed to the door, and even before she was through it Jake was talking on the phone. "Sorry to keep you. Yes, it's all in hand. You'll have delivery in about . . ."

Closing the door, she made her way back across the street to the turning shop. But she found it quite impossible to focus her mind on work, and decided on an early lunch break. Buying a sandwich and some fruit, she took it to eat on a bench on the esplanade. A few boats skimmed the glittering water of the bay, most of them under sail, and she felt a surge of happy anticipation. Tomorrow, she'd be out there with Jake. Her heartbeat quickened and a wash of heat flooded through her body at the thought of his lips on hers, his hands caressing her soft flesh. The way she felt now, tomorrow seemed a long time to wait.

There was a small boutique in the hotel foyer, and Lee stopped in before it closed to buy suitable gear for tomorrow. Jake had said to wear something casual, but there was casual and casual. She had no intention of appearing in the floppy, shapeless garments sailing people often wore. The young shop assistant was friendly and ready to help. When Lee explained that she was after something smart, but still practical for sailing, the girl produced stretch denim jeans and a very stylish blue-and-white matelot sweater. Fortunately, Lee was a stock size and both garments fitted her to perfection. The girl had just produced a scarlet parka to complete the outfit when another woman entered the shop. Around thirty, she was a real svelte beauty, with a creamy complexion and wavy raven-black hair that hung down her back in a gleaming dark waterfall. She walked straight through the shop with an air of assurance, calling, "Come into the office, Gwynneth. I want to talk to you."

"But I'm serving, Miss Channon," the girl protested.

The woman swung 'round and Lee found herself being

measured with coolly contemptuous appraisal. "Heavens above, Gwynneth, I only need you for a couple of minutes. Come on!"

"Would you mind very much?" the assistant whispered to Lee.

"No, that's okay. These things are fine, so I'll go back to the cubicle and get changed."

Left alone, Lee could hear the murmur of voices, chiefly the newcomer's. She appeared to be giving a string of brusque instructions. Then, fully ten minutes later, she swept through the shop again without so much as a glance at Lee.

"I . . . I'm terribly sorry to have kept you waiting," the girl said as she came hurrying back, flustered.

"Your boss?" Lee queried, deciding to be amused rather than annoyed.

"That's right. Actually, her father owns a chain of hotels like this one, and Miss Channon has a boutique in most of them. Real goldmines, if you ask me, because as far as I know she doesn't pay a penny rent or anything."

"Some people," Lee observed as she started to write out a check, "have all the luck."

"Usually the ones who least deserve it." The girl slapped a guilty hand to her mouth. "Oh dear, I'm afraid that sort of slipped out."

Lee grinned reassuringly. "It's okay, my lips are sealed."

Upstairs in her room, showering before changing for another solitary dinner, she decided on an impulse to try on her sailing outfit again. She studied her reflection in the long mirror. Not bad, not bad at all. She clasped her arms and fingered the smooth material of the windproof parka. A swift sensation of Jake's hands upon her flashed into her mind . . . hands that touched her body freely in an erotic exultation of her feminine beauty. Because he *did* think her beautiful; he'd said so. She sighed with wistful rapture. Jake Talbot was surely the most perfect lover imaginable, an exciting, generous lover whose first and foremost consideration would be to give pleasure to his partner. His partner . . . whoever that might happen to be, she thought, a *frisson* of sadness whispering through her. Last Sunday it had been Lee Jordan, and in between . . . who? She laughed shakily to herself as she changed into a cinnamon-colored dress with a wide leather belt. If I'm not careful, she told her reflection, I'll start to fall in love with the man. And that will never do.

The knowledge that she already loved Jake was securely locked away in the most secret compartment of Lee's heart, to which no part of her conscious mind was permitted a key.

The expression of warm approval in Jake's eyes as Lee met him in the hotel lobby next morning repaid all the trouble she'd taken with her appearance. He took her hand and held it tightly as they went out and down the steps together to his waiting car.

"You look fantastic, out of this world," he told her as they drove off. "Those close-fitting jeans would make any man's mind boggle, imagining what lies underneath. But I'm lucky. I don't need a vivid imagination in that direction—I know."

She blushed, and didn't mind his seeing. "I bought them yesterday at the boutique in the hotel," she explained. "Not having come prepared to go sailing."

"So Merle Channon came up trumps."

"Channon? She's the one who owns the boutique?"

Jake nodded. "And a number of others besides. Quite an enterprising businesswoman is Merle Channon."

"You know her, do you?" Lee queried. There had been something in his tone that caused her to wonder.

"In Aberdyffryn," he replied lightly, "everyone knows

everyone else." Then, "Were you served by Merle herself?"

"No, but she came into the shop while I was there."

"Oh, I see." Jake flickered her a sideways glance. "How did you get on with her?"

"We didn't speak," Lee told him, and thought it best to say no more. But her mind was busy with speculation.

In a few moments they reached the marina, and Jake turned in at the entrance. He drove past the clubhouse, a seafood restaurant and a row of stores selling all kinds of gear for boating before finding a vacant parking space.

There was activity all around as they got out of the car and walked across the quayside, Jake carrying the picnic hamper, and he exchanged greetings with several people he knew. For a few moments he and Lee stood at the water's edge, looking down at the lines of boats that were berthed on either side of floating pontoons. A number of them were sleek motor cruisers, she noticed, but for the most part they were sailboats of different sizes and shapes. As they rocked gently, the tall masts and rigging made a delicate tracery against the almost cloudless blue sky.

"Which is your boat, Jake?" she asked.

He pointed. "The one at the end there, on the left, with the dark-blue hull."

"What's her name?" Lee screwed up her eyes to read the lettering on the prow. *"Lancashire Lass."*

"She was originally built as a fishing boat," Jake explained. "A prawner. That must have been around the turn of the century. From the little information I've been able to scrape together she led a busy working life in Morecambe Bay. But she was eventually retired to the scrap heap in a Liverpool breaker's yard. That's where I rescued her."

"And you had her repaired?"

"Had her repaired? Do you mind!"

"You mean you did it yourself?"

Jake nodded. "Down to every last nail and lick of paint. Come on and let me show you."

They made their way along the floating pontoon to the far end, and stepped down onto the deck of the *Lancashire Lass,* which dipped slightly under their weight. Lee glanced around her with keen interest. Though built on much sturdier lines than modern yachts designed for racing, she was still a graceful craft. And everything down to the smallest detail was immaculately finished . . . the timbering varnished to the smoothness of glass, the paintwork gleaming and the wheel of solid oak studded with polished brass. "You did a marvelous job, Jake," she exclaimed. "It's beautiful."

"So are you," he said softly from behind her.

Lee felt excitement pulse through her as she turned to look at him. She was met by the intent gaze of his dark eyes, which glowed with a blatant sensuality that seemed to burn into her. Consciously, Lee made an effort to throw off the shadow that had lain across her happiness since the name Merle Channon had come up. This was *her* day, and it was stupid to let it be spoiled by the thought of other women in Jake's life.

"Let me show you the cabin," he said, holding out his hand to her.

They stepped down from the deck into the cockpit, then down three steps into the cabin. It was roomy, with four bunks, a fixed table and bench seats covered in orange leather. Lee could easily stand upright, but she noted that Jake's head only just avoided touching the roof.

"It's really super," she said, determinedly chatty, the warm contact of his fingers making her bloodcells tingle. "I love this furniture and the color scheme. It's easy to see the hand of an expert designer."

"Oh, I'm an expert designer, all right." Jake laughed, gathering her into his arms. "Right now I've got designs on you, Lee."

"Is there . . . is there a galley?" she stammered, feeling herself going weak at the knees.

"You name it . . . it's here," he said with a gesture of dismissal. "You'll have plenty of time later for a tour of inspection. At this moment, I want to kiss you rather urgently."

As his lips came to meet hers, Lee felt a dizzy sense of delight—of relief—at once again knowing the heaven of his embrace. She melted against his rock-hard body and slid her arms up to clasp tightly around his neck. For long, lovely moments they stood locked together, swaying with the gentle movement of the boat. She felt Jake's quickened heartbeat thudding against her own, felt the heat of him burning through their clothes, felt the trembling of his passion in the hands that roamed over her slender shape.

But . . . there were people around. She heard a family party arrive at the very next boat, jumping aboard with lots of laughter and chitchat.

"Jake . . ." she protested, trying to press back from him.

"What's the matter, sweetheart?" His voice was thick, and she knew that he was already almost lost in the intensity of his desire.

"Shouldn't we . . . hadn't we better be getting under way?" she blurted.

"Who cares?" he muttered distractedly as his fingers raked across her back and found the sensitive hollows of her spine.

"We're supposed to be having a sail," she reminded him, feeling her determination draining away with every passing second.

"Oh that . . . yes, I suppose so." He kissed her again on the lips, then trailed his mouth lingeringly across her jaw and down the curve of her neck before reluctantly letting her go.

Back in the cockpit, Jake started the auxiliary engine, then he cast off the mooring lines. Under power, *Lancashire Lass* backed its way slowly from the pontoon, and then Jake swung her 'round. When they were clear of other boats, he opened the throttle and they passed out of the marina into the open water of the bay.

It was a glorious morning, all freshness and loveliness —really warm for late September. The sea was like a shimmering sheet of silver gilt. Lee stood on deck, her hand gripping a polished brass rail, and reveled in the soft, ozone-tangy air that brushed silkily past her face, teasing out stray tendrils of her honey-blond hair that she'd tied back with a braided black ribbon.

"Kick off those sandals of yours," Jake advised from his place behind the wheel. "You'll be more comfortable with bare feet."

She did so, and enjoyed the feel of spreading her toes on the satin-smooth planking. The scarlet parka, which she'd already unzipped against the growing heat of the day, she now slipped off altogether and laid aside, smoothing the matelot sweater over her hips. Jake emitted a drawn-out wolf whistle.

"Chauvinist!" she retorted, sticking out her tongue at him.

"Can I help it if you have that effect on me?"

She suppressed a smile, and asked, "Is it okay for me to wander around on the deck, Jake?"

"Feel free. As long as you don't fall overboard." He trimmed the throttle slightly. "Come to think of it, though, that would give me an opportunity for a gallant rescue, so please go ahead."

"And ruin my new jeans?"

"You'd look like a beautiful mermaid," Jake mused. "Your clothes would cling wetly to your sexy curves, with

68

your gorgeous hair streaming out behind. We could make love in the briny depths." He sighed heavily. "What a fantastic way to drown!"

Lee tilted her head and gazed up at the tall mast. "Aren't you going to hoist the sails?"

"Not yet. What little wind there is happens to be dead against us at the moment, and it would take forever to get a few miles out." He patted the engine housing. "I'd rather use a lazy man's sails."

"Pity! I was hoping to fill a gap in my education and learn something about seamanship and navigation."

"I'll give you a lesson later on," he promised.

"How and when did you learn yourself?"

"When I was a teenager. I had a fine tutor, a retired fisherman who was a real old salt. What Morgan Jones didn't know about handling a boat wasn't worth knowing."

Lee cautiously moved forward along the deck above the cabin and went to stand in the pointed prow. With her feet wedged against the low wooden bulwark, she took a firm grip on a stay rope. There was something hypnotic in the gentle movement of the boat, the steady wash of the bow wave, the creak of the rigging, the unbroken pulse of the engine. She drifted off into a fantasy in which the world was left behind and she and Jake sailed the smooth sunlit seas in a voyage that continued forever. . . .

The light touch of his hands on her shoulders caused her to jerk out of her dream.

"You . . . you startled me."

"Sorry. It's time for your sailing lesson."

"Oh . . . oh yes, of course."

He still held her by the shoulders, and his hands began a slow massaging movement that sent swirls of blissful sensation flurrying through her.

"If you'd prefer a lesson in another subject," he

murmured into her hair, "you'll find that I'm very versatile as a teacher."

She laughed and pulled away from him. "I think we'd better stick to sailing."

"Right, then. Lesson one—how to sail close to the wind."

Lee gave him a cautious look, suspecting a tease.

"Since the wind is blowing shoreward," he explained, "which is dead opposite the way we want the boat to go, we'll have to 'beat to windward.' Come on, we'll get the sails up and I'll show you."

For the next half-hour or so Lee became absorbed in the fascinating process of making a boat respond to instructions and not follow its own inclinations. Jake let her make mistakes, then corrected her quietly. Her main fault was being too gentle in putting the helm over when changing tack on their zigzag course, so that *Lancashire Lass* became "caught in stays," which meant pointing into the wind and drifting slowly backward.

At length Jake said, "That's enough sailing instruction for one afternoon. I think we'll be okay to drop anchor here."

After consulting the chart and checking the echo sounder, he put the bow into the wind. When the boat lost headway he cast the anchor and let out the chain. Then he lowered the sails. "Right, Lee, that's it. We can forget about the boat now, and concentrate on each other."

Lee held her breath as he jumped down into the cockpit and took her into his arms, seeking her mouth eagerly and pressing his long lean length hard against her. She responded to him without hesitation, her arms sliding up to twine about his neck and pull his head down in a deeper kiss. His tongue thrust in, a welcome invader, and then withdrew—tantalizingly, temptingly, invitingly.

Lee boldly accepted the challenge, letting the sensitive tip of her tongue savor the taste of his lips, tracing the even line of his teeth, exploring deeper to coil thrillingly against his tongue. Jake's heart and hers joined in a thudding drumbeat of desire that obliterated all other sound. They were acutely aware of each other's touch, the other's warmth, the other's vibrant longing. Today, Lee hadn't any doubts that she wanted Jake to make love to her.

The sun, mounting ever higher in the sky, shone down on them warmly, and the zephyr breeze was an added caress on their skin. Jake's lips feathered her cheek, brushed over the smoothness of her brow, and he nuzzled his face deeply into her hair. He tugged loose the restraining ribbon with an impatient hand so that her hair tumbled free, streaming out and gleaming in the sunlight like a silken mane, and he ran his fingers through it sensuously. Lee tilted her head back so that she could lay her mouth against his throat, pressing little kisses around the curve of his thrustful jawline, lingering at the cleft of his chin until, with a shuddering groan of passion, Jake locked his lips on hers again in another drowning kiss.

"Oh Lee . . . wonderful, beautiful, exciting Lee," he murmured hoarsely as he drew back at last. His dark eyes gazed down into the clear sapphire depths of hers with a question. An unvoiced question which she answered without the need for words. Jake stepped up from the cockpit to the level deck above the cabin, then bent to help her clamber over the coaming to join him. All around them the sea was empty, the only sign of life an occasional wheeling gull. Toward the distant shoreline, a number of sails could be seen, and in the other direction, far out to sea, was a smudge of smoke from a large vessel following a shipping lane. Here they were alone with the warm sun and blue sky and the soft slap of water against the hull. As much alone, Lee reflected, as in his mountain cottage, cut off by a blanketing fog. Remembering that night, she felt a shiver of excitement flurry through her body, and Jake noticed.

"You can't be cold?" he queried, lifting a thick eyebrow in amusement.

"Heavens no!" She gave a nervous laugh. "Rather the reverse, actually. The sun is quite hot, isn't it?"

A slow smile spread across his lean features. "Luckily, being overwarm is a condition that's easily remedied."

Still standing, Jake proceeded to undress her. With the matelot sweater removed, he paused to ripple his fingertips over the soft skin covering her ribcage before homing in on the snap fastener of her jeans. The zip slithered open and the hip-hugging garment slid down, his hands assisting, until, around her ankles, she could step free of it.

Jake sighed deeply, and smiled at her. "This is the moment I've been dreaming of. It's been dangling before me tantalizingly, driving me crazy, ever since last Sunday. I've tried to hold your sublime beauty in my imagination, and inevitably failed. No mental picture can be as wonderful as the reality."

With his two palms pressed to her thighs, he kneaded and stroked the firm silky flesh, his fingertips tracing swirling patterns on her skin that sent desire racing through her and turned her bones to water. Then his hands moved upward around her slender hips and into the inward curve of her back, and upward further until they reached the fastening of her bra. In an instant it was open, the wisp of lace fabric falling away, his hands coming 'round to claim her breasts, cupping their soft roundness as he bent to bury his face in the secret, fragrant valley between them.

Slowly, Jake raised his head until his dark eyes were gazing directly into hers with smoldering passion. His voice was low and thick. "Lee, you lovely, lovely creature. I want to make love to you and go on making love to you neverendingly, all day long."

Did she actually cry out yes, yes, yes? Or was the clamor only in her eager mind?

When Jake dropped to his knees on the deck, she suddenly felt shy to be standing naked in the open air without the shield of his body, and she raised an arm to cover her breasts. But Jake at once protested, drawing her arm away.

"There's no one to see, sweetheart, and I won't allow you to hide yourself from me."

Still kneeling before her, his hands came to rest on the waistband of her panties, drawing them over her hips and down her legs with agonizing slowness, his gaze upon her in reverential adoration, his arms encircling her and his fingers clenching with tender savagery into the soft roundness of her buttocks. Lee cried out as desire spiraled within her and she jerked convulsively, her hands grasping blindly for Jake, coaxing him up to a standing position again. She clasped him to her in a frenzy of sensual excitement.

Several exquisite minutes later, with her eyes tightly closed, she felt him move back from her. She opened her eyes again to find him gazing at her with a strange look of appeal. And then she understood, understood his need. Naked as she was, she started in her turn to divest him of his clothes. First the thick-knit blue shirt, opening it button by button from neck to navel, then she inserted her hands to roam wantonly across the smooth-muscled contours of his chest, lightly drawing her fingernails across the resilient, bronzed skin, glorying in his gasp of arousal, wickedly teasing the small, pebble-hard male nipples . . . until she, as much as he, could bear the delicious torment no longer and she quickly dragged out his shirt from the restraining waistband and pulled it away from him. Jake reached out for her with urgent hands, but she made him permit her to take her fill of drinking in the beauty of his body, as he had done with her. Then, with a soft sigh, she urged him to kneel with her and pressed him backwards until his bare shoulders lay against the deck, and ran a line of butterfly kisses from his throat down to where the flat flesh of his belly disappeared beneath his belted jeans.

Jake groaned loudly, shudderingly. "Lee . . . my darling Lee, I can't . . . I can't wait. . . ."

She grinned down at him impishly, intoxicated by her sudden accession of power over him. "Yes, you can. You will, if I say so."

She touched the brass belt buckle, fingering its metallic smoothness, then slowly and deliberately opened it. The metal clip of his jeans came in for her attention next, a long, delightful moment flickering by as Lee pulled it gently apart. She took the tab of his zipper and eased it downward a single inch, putting the coolness of her lips to the vee of tanned skin she'd newly exposed. Another inch, another tiny kiss. And yet again. Then with a relenting laugh she finished in fleeting seconds the task she had been so long about, pulling away the jeans and the minimal briefs he wore beneath them so that he lay outstretched before her quite naked. Awed by the perfect symmetry of his long-limbed body, the satiny texture of taut skin rippling over hard muscles, Lee gazed at him in silent wonderment.

Jake was staring back at her with hot, tortured eyes. A groan broke from his lips, and his whole body shuddered. "Lee . . . for God's sake . . . touch me!" he pleaded.

Hesitantly, with a sudden onset of shyness, she moved her hand slowly and did as he bid. Jake's body convulsed in a violent jerk as her caressing fingers met his sensitive flesh, suede-soft, yet hard and pulsing with the burning heat of passion. Lee felt a wave of tender emotion that sweetly suffused her whole being. Giving a low moan, she sank down to lie beside him on the sun-warmed planks of the deck, and Jake reached out his arms and drew her close.

The sun inched across the deep blue sky, beaming its golden light upon the two entwined bodies as they rapturously made love. Jake reverenced her with his hands, trailing his mouth in an erotic journey of tiny skimming kisses. As his questing lips reached hers, she seized his head and returned the kiss with a sweet, yearning savagery, their two mouths stretched wide, their tongues meeting together, thrusting and twisting and curling in an abandonment of sensual delight. He rolled onto his back again and drew Lee above him, holding her poised there by his steel-strong arms so that the soft ripeness of her breasts hung in reach of his eager mouth. She gasped in joyous torment as he circled their coned shape with the pointed tip of his tongue, and almost sobbed when he fastened his lips over a nipple, swollen and hard with the wild blaze of her passion. For delirious minutes on end he nipped and tugged and softly caressed her breasts with his warm, moist mouth, while his body writhed beneath her in a battle for self-control.

Then, gently, but with swift certainty that this was the right moment, Jake moved her to lie beside him again, and the warmth of the planking was smooth to her naked skin. He slid a hand downward over the long curve of her hip and between the soft flesh of her thighs, urging them to part. Her body throbbed in excited anticipation as his hand moved purposefully upward, and she gave an involuntary shudder that was something like dread at the tormenting ecstasy he was intent on bringing her.

"You're so beautiful," he whispered huskily. "So soft and lovely. You're everything that is most wonderful in a woman. My sweet Lee, do I please you? Do I make you happy?"

Her joyful yes was a half-articulate sound smothered by the thickness in her throat. In a daze of sensual delight she felt herself floating heavenward, soaring ever higher toward the sun's golden ball. Soon all awareness of everything else was gone but for the gilded radiance of pure sensation as Jake, touching her body lovingly with his hands, carried her from high peak to even higher peak, each seeming surely to be the ultimate before the final blissful explosion . . . on and on while she cried and moaned and clawed blindly at him, rocking her body in raptured frenzy until, when it seemed that her very mind and reason must desert her if this terrifying sweetness didn't end, the sun itself shattered into fragments and poured down in a stream of glorious golden lava, and her sobs of ecstasy were stifled by Jake's lips upon hers.

An eon of time drifted by as Lee's reflexive shuddering quieted until she lay still and warm in the cherishing circle of Jake's arms. When at long last she let her eyelids flutter open, the image of his face was spangled by her tears. Gently, he touched his lips to each eye in turn, kissing the tears away. She saw, surprisingly, that Jake's dark eyes were also glistening, and she realized that he had been intensely moved by the wondrous experience he had given her.

He drew her closer, his hands moving up to sink into her silken hair, his lips finding the soft welcome of her mouth. The desire Lee had believed to be assuaged curled once more in her loins at the insistent vibrant pressure of his need against her. She smiled an invitation to him mistily, and opened herself to him. With a long, juddering sigh Jake slid into her, his mouth closing over hers, his hands roaming her body, pausing at the soft mounds of her buttocks and clenching there as the two of them moved together in their mutual journey to paradise. Even now, even when desire must be raging within him like a fiery furnace, he paced himself to her, exerting iron self-control, enticing her onward once more toward the wild abandonment where ecstasy lay. She felt the whole length of his hard body shake and tremble as he neared the peak, step by step with her. With tense, rigid fingers she tore at his dark hair, raked his back and threshed about in mounting joy. And the sun splintered once again and poured down its golden rain as, with a hoarse cry, Jake shuddered in a last paroxysm and finally became still, breath rasping in his throat.

His weight was upon her and the hard deck beneath. But Lee found happiness in her discomfort, drawing him down more heavily to the cushion of her body.

"Sweet . . . sweet darling Lee," he murmured. "It was wonderful, fantastic. Was it for you?"

"Yes," she whispered shyly. "Oh Jake, I can't tell you how wonderful."

He moved then so that he could carry the burden of her weight. Lee curled against his smooth warm flesh, and with a single fingertip gently and lovingly drew the outline of his features . . . eyes, nose, mouth; around the angular curve of his strong jaw, feeling the pulse throbbing in the hollow of his throat. Together, they dozed off, drifting into a beautiful, relaxed quiescence.

4

As Lee drifted back to awareness and let her eyelids flutter open, she found that Jake was gazing down at her tenderly. He touched his lips to hers, and the gentle pressure evoked thrilling echoes of the passion they had shared.

"Thank you, darling," he said softly.

Lee pressed a scolding finger to his lips. "Remember what you said in your office yesterday? Everything between us is mutual, shared, equal. So if you thank me, Jake, I have to thank you just as much."

Nodding, he squeezed her arm in acknowledgment of the pact. "And now," he said, "my equal stomach is crying out for sustenance."

"I'm hungry, too," she admitted with a smile. "I'll get dressed."

Jake caught her hand. "I don't want you to get dressed."

"If I don't cover up, I'll burn."

He slanted her a look. "Do you have any suntan lotion in your handbag?"

"Yes, but . . ."

"Give it to me, then, and I'll apply a protective coating all over this ravishing body of yours."

She found the thought incredibly exciting. Shrugging, she said, "If you think it's worth the trouble."

"Worth the trouble?" His voice rang with incredulity. "Listen, I'll fetch a rug and some cushions, so you can relax. Don't go away."

A couple of minutes later Lee was lying face down on the plaid rug, while Jake poured some lotion from the bottle into his palm and smoothed it across her back. He worked carefully, methodically, spreading it around her neck and shoulders, down to her waist and buttocks, her thighs and calves. She reveled in the friction of his hands passing over her skin, and gasped aloud with pleasurable excitement when he bent to plant kisses on the back of her knees.

"Right, turn over," he said presently, giving her a playful slap on the bottom.

Lee felt oddly vulnerable lying there with her body stretched out before him as he knelt over her. The lotion-spreading massage began again, even more sensuous now, becoming frankly erotic as he dealt meticulously with the rosy peak of each breast, the little hollow of her navel; lower down came blissful intimacies which made her writhe and moan in tormented joy.

"Stop, Jake . . . please stop."

But it was quite some time before Jake at last brought the sweet torture to an end, and said, "Now we'll switch places. You can do the same for me."

Lee laughed as she sat up. "You don't really need protection from the sun, Jake. Your skin is beautifully tanned as it is. Still, if that's what you want."

Strange that she should feel so shy about ministering to

him . . . the man with whom she'd just been making love in a fever of passion. She poured lotion and smoothed it onto the firm flesh of his chest, across the muscled shoulders, the strong column of his neck, down the tapered length of his arms.

"There, that's done."

Catching her hand, he pulled it down and placed it against the taut flat plane of his abdomen. "You haven't finished yet, Lee."

"Oh, yes I have!" But even as she spoke, her eager fingers began to caress him again in a slow, curling, downward motion. Then she stopped herself.

"That's enough, Jake," she said in a voice that was tense with emotion.

"Not nearly enough," he corrected. "But okay . . . we'll call a halt and eat now." He pushed himself up on his elbows, and lingered to give her a pulse-stopping kiss on the lips before scrambling to his feet. Stepping down into the cockpit, he vanished into the cabin beneath the deck, while Lee sat hugging her knees, gazing over the bulwark at the empty stretch of shimmering water all around them. She felt like purring, she was so happy.

Jake reappeared almost at once carrying the picnic hamper and a bottle of wine he'd had cooling in the fridge. He arranged the cushions against the cockpit coaming so they could rest back comfortably, then drew the cork and filled just one glass, which they shared sip for sip. The wine was cool and refreshing, leaving a faint prickle on the palate. She tasted its nutty flavor again on Jake's lips as he turned to kiss her.

"I got this grub at the delicatessen near my flat," he said as they opened the hamper. "I hope it'll be okay."

"It smells wonderful," Lee said, suddenly ravenous.

Together they unpacked the food, spreading it around them, removing lids from the various containers. There was chicken and some spicy little sausages, crisp salad and crusty bread. Between them they made big inroads into the plentiful supplies, and finished up with fruit, Jake feeding her with grapes between kisses.

When they'd both had enough, they lay back contentedly, arms and legs entwined as in the afterglow of making love. The sun, scarcely past its zenith, was deliciously warm on their bare skin, its heat tempered by the silken brushing of the westerly breeze.

"A day to be remembered," Jake murmured softly. "A day when everything seems to go right, perfect and unflawed."

Lee thrust aside the uneasy thought that to him this was just an unusually good day in the course of his life. That was all it should be to her, too, she thought determinedly. What more did she expect, or even want?

"Perfect," she agreed in a drowsy whisper.

He kissed her, lightly and lingeringly, on the mouth. A kiss that suddenly became more passionate with the quickening pressure of his body. With a nervous little laugh Lee pushed him back, almost scared by the swiftness of her own reawakened desire. A burning heat flooded through her, and her heart was thudding.

"You . . . you certainly have a lovely boat," she faltered.

"Yes, she is lovely," Jake agreed solemnly. "Outstandingly lovely. She has a strong will, yet she responds gratifyingly to my every desire. She has class, breeding, beauty, intelligence. . . ."

"All that in a boat?" Lee queried with a shaky laugh.

Jake had the whole time been looking directly into her eyes. "Oh yes, of course, it's the boat we're supposed to be talking about."

"Why are boats always referred to as 'she'?" Lee demanded quickly.

"Good question. Like a woman, a boat can be everything that's wonderful. Soft and gentle and yielding.

Then suddenly she'll show you she has a will of her own, and she exerts it."

"That sounds suspiciously like a sexist remark."

"Garbage," he replied inelegantly.

"Huh! The usual dismissal of argument by a male who finds himself cornered," she remarked sarcastically.

"To hear you say that," Jake responded, "and despite today's evidence to the contrary, anyone would think you didn't like men."

"Put it this way . . . men aren't as perfect as they choose to think."

"I'm not perfect?" he queried in mock astonishment.

"Now you're doing what men always accuse women of doing . . . turning a generalization into something personal."

"I'm relieved to hear," he countered with a grin, "that you weren't referring to me. So tell me about the faults of the other men in your life. Ashley Hammond, for example."

"Ashley is not—" Lee closed her mouth against what she had been about to spill out—that Ashley was merely her business partner, not "a man in her life." Instinct warned her that it would be better to let Jake go on thinking there was something between herself and Ashley. If he knew the truth—that there wasn't any other man, and hadn't been since Stephen—he would become even more confident of his power over her. When the time came (and Lee made herself face the fact that it must come very soon) for this tempestuous, white-hot romance between her and Jake to end, she wanted to be able to walk away with her pride intact, without his guessing that the days and months ahead would be like a bleak, desert wilderness.

On a counter train of thought she longed to be honest with Jake, to confess to him that since her husband had died she'd allowed no other man to make love to her. But that would be too revealing, if she wanted to save her pride. It was vital for her to retain a degree of control over what happened between them, not just be swept along on the tidal wave of her emotions.

If she had not taken the wrong turning in the fog last Sunday, she mused, things would have turned out very differently. Suppose she could step back in time and put herself that day on the right road to Aberdyffryn, so that she would never have known Jake except as a client. Given the choice, would she do so? Her reasoning brain tried to insist on an unequivocal "yes," but her wayward heart gave a different answer.

Jake flicked the tip of her nose with a reminding finger. "Hey, wake up, Lee! You were saying that Ashley Hammond is not—what?"

"I'll tell you what he *is*," she riposted, giving herself a mental shake. "Ashley is a basically kind man, thoughtful, considerate and generous. As well as being a really first-class architect."

"Quite a paragon. I notice, though, that you didn't mention his rating as a lover."

"Naturally not," she said, after a moment of quick thinking. "Would *you* want to discuss . . . other women?"

Jake grinned at her. "If that was meant as a floater, sweetheart, you can be reassured. I don't kiss and tell, so you're quite safe." For a moment his face grew somber, then suddenly he scrambled to his feet, towering above her, tall and magnificent in his nakedness. "Come on, let's have a swim."

"Is it safe for us both to leave the boat?"

"Sure. I've put the swimming ladder down for us to get back." Crouching, he gathered her into his arms and carried her to the side, then held her suspended over the rippling blue water. "Shall I throw you in?"

"If you like," she said recklessly.

"No doubt you swim like a fish?"

"Put it this way, I'm not gold medalist material. But neither am I likely to drown."

Jake didn't throw her in. Instead, he stepped up onto the bulwark with her still held close in his arms, and jumped. They entered the water with a mighty splash and sank amid foaming bubbles into the iridescent depths. His arms went around her and his mouth sought hers, fastening to it hungrily. When they broke surface a moment later, the sun spangling in spectrum colors that dazzled Lee's eyes, they were kissing with wild passion. With a gurgling laugh, she broke away and struck out strongly in a fast crawl. But Jake had caught her again within a few strokes, his arms circling her from behind, his hands clasping upon her breasts, his legs firmly clamping hers. Inevitably, they began to sink again. Lee felt his teeth nibbling into her neck.

For nearly half an hour they gamboled in the sun-bright water, never more than a few yards from the boat, swimming a little, playing and wrestling a little, some-times clinging to the ladder for a brief rest. And often, as passion overwhelmed them, clinching together in long, salt-tasting kisses.

At length they clambered aboard *Lancashire Lass* again, their bodies streaming water, Lee's hair clinging wet about her shoulders. And while the warm sun dried them, they made love once more . . . made love with uninhibited passion. Lee made a gift to him of her body, and in exchange Jake turned every caress, every quest-ing movement of his hands and lips and tongue into an act of worship of her beauty, carrying her upward into a rarefied atmosphere in which every breath she took was tingling with champagne bubbles, higher and higher until the sun blazed before her with a pure white incandescent light, and the heavens erupted in a blaze of shimmering glory. They both gave a shuddering cry of exultation. Then came the slow descent till they were silent and still, suffused with warm loveliness. Presently she felt Jake's hand begin a tender exploration that awoke faint, rippling echoes of their shared ecstasy.

"Darling Lee," he murmured huskily. "What a wonderful, wonderful woman you are! It's impossible to imagine that making love could ever be a more glorious experience."

"Oh, Jake," she whispered, pressing her open palm to the warm flesh of his cheek, then running her fingertips lightly down the curving line of his jaw and throat. "Oh, Jake!"

She fell into a golden dream, always happily conscious of his body curled against hers, his strong, steady heartbeat, his idly caressing hand. In her misty fantasy they remained there together forever, the small sailboat on an empty sea their own private heaven, and made love throughout all eternity.

But at long last, when Lee was becoming aware of the first faint touch of chill in the breeze that stroked her skin, Jake stirred. "I'm afraid," he said regretfully, "it's time for us to get dressed and return to harbor."

"Must we?" she murmured, still clinging to her dream.

He sat up beside her and let his hand run a sensuous trail down her body, from her shoulder across the mound of her breasts and over the soft flesh of her abdomen, pausing to tease her navel and then the full slender length of her legs. And all the while he held her gaze, smiling seductively deep into her eyes.

"Don't tempt me, woman," he said with a heartfelt sigh. He reached to where their clothes were piled in an untidy heap, and picked up her wispy bra. "Now we've got to cover up these lovely, tantalizing breasts. But I shall remember how sexy they make me feel when I look at them, how deliciously exciting it is to hold their beautiful weight in my hands . . . how I can make you writhe and moan with pleasure when I touch them and . . ."

"Don't," she said faintly.

He slipped the bra on, taking his time about it, and finally hooked the clasp. "There," he said smugly, as if he'd performed a major feat of precision engineering. "Now for these panties, designed expressly to inflame a man's imagination."

"It would appear that your imagination doesn't need any inflaming," she teased, darting him a bold look.

Jake glanced back at her, his dark eyes glinting wickedly. "Didn't I tell you not to tempt me? Now, for goodness' sake stand up and get these on you." Lee did as he instructed, stepping into the panties and adjusting them around her slim waist. Then he pressed his lips to what they covered. "Out of sight, but not out of mind," he declared. "Jeans next. Then your sweater . . ."

Fully dressed, she ran raking fingers through her now-dry hair. It felt sticky and she knew that she'd be able to do little with it until she could wash out the sea salt. The ribbon she'd worn was in the pocket of her jeans, so she tied her hair back as best she could.

Already Jake was tugging on his own jeans, zipping them up. In another moment he was into his thick-knit blue shirt and had buttoned it up. "How about you making us some coffee while I get underway," he suggested.

"Aye-aye, cap'n," she said, saluting him with a grin, and she disappeared below.

As they skimmed before a freshening breeze toward the bay where Aberdyffryn nestled in a fold of surrounding hills, the glow of the setting sun threw crimson banners across the sea and turned *Lancashire Lass*'s sails to fiery gold. Scanning this magnificent display of color,

Jake commented, "It looks as if tomorrow will be just as fine as today. I'd like nothing better than to spend it with you, sweetheart . . . in an exact rerun of today. You can't improve on perfection, can you? But . . ."

Lee waited, her breath caught with anxiety.

". . . but it's impossible, I'm afraid. In fact," he added with an apologetic smile, "I'll have to leave you as soon as I've dropped you back at the hotel."

"You mean you have a . . ."—she almost said "date," but amended it to—" . . . an appointment?"

He nodded. "I was invited for the whole weekend, actually, but I managed to postpone my arrival until this evening. I'd have ducked out altogether if I could, but the people concerned are big customers, Lee."

"Oh, it's business!" Marginally, this tempered her bitter disappointment.

Standing at the wheel with his arm around her waist, Jake drew her harder against his lean frame. "Don't sound so scathing about business," he scolded laughingly. "Even in your highflown profession of architecture I expect you find it necessary to do a little socializing now and then."

"Well, yes," she admitted. "Only . . ."

"I know, darling." He nodded, his mouth tightening into a hard, straight line. "It's a darned shame that it has to be *this* weekend. There's so little time left for us to be together that it's hell losing tonight and all day tomorrow."

For Lee, the freshening breeze seemed suddenly to have become a cold, relentless wind. Pulling herself away from him, she went to fetch her parka. Till that moment, the shape of their future relationship had remained hazy in her mind. Even after she returned home at the end of next week—assuming, of course, that Jake accepted the proposals she and Ashley submitted to him—she would often have cause to visit Aberdyffryn over a prolonged period while the extensions to the factory were completed. Vaguely, without spelling it out to herself, she had envisioned a continuing affair with Jake in the months ahead. That it would have to end sometime, she had accepted from the start, knowing his general outlook on life . . . a hedonistic philosophy of grabbing one's chances, of taking what was offered. But it was clear from the way Jake had just spoken that in his view, when they said good-bye next weekend, their passionate affair would be over. For him, it would be another pleasant memory of some good sex. For her . . . what? One thing she knew with utter certainty, she would never forget Jake Talbot. He would remain, always and forever, the yardstick by which she judged every other man.

With her parka on, she didn't return to stand by Jake, but sat on the opposite side of the cockpit looking back at the foaming wake which echoed the flaring colors of the western sky . . . carmine by that time, with great swathes of orange and scarlet. Why couldn't she, Lee pondered regretfully, take the same cool, unemotional view of their relationship as Jake did . . . a brief, idyllic encounter with a definite time span? For her, though, it was unique and cataclysmic. No man had ever possessed the power to stir her senses the way Jake had done. Their day had been wonderful, fantastic, more exciting than she'd ever imagined it possible for lovemaking to be. How could she view the bliss she'd known in Jake's arms as completely fulfilling in itself, with no thought of the future? How could she part with Jake at the end of next week accepting that their affair had been a brief, happy episode which had run its course? Another seven days and she would inevitably feel an ever deeper sense of committing herself to him; every hour and every minute they were together would make it more impossible for her to close the door on their special relationship without pain and anguish. Jake might blithely call a halt next weekend, but for herself . . . she knew unhappily that it wouldn't be the end. She would continue to love him.

Love. Once set free in her brain, the word echoed and reechoed. Yes, she loved Jake. Had loved him, of course, from the very first moment he'd confronted her at the cottage. How else could she have behaved in such an abandoned fashion that night? Only from love, she realized now, and marveled that she could hitherto have blinded herself to this plain and simple truth.

The revelation, though, brought her no happiness. It was something she could not share with Jake, nor with anyone else. She must keep it locked within her heart as a dark secret.

From his place at the wheel, Jake called, "Why are you looking so gloomy, sweetheart? Come over here by me."

Unwillingly, her pulses leaping, Lee stood up and went to join him. At once Jake put his arm around her and drew her close, pulling her hip against his thigh, her head against his shoulder.

In a rush of panic that he might start kissing her again, Lee sought around for an impersonal topic of conversation. "Er . . . who's this client you're going to see?"

Was there the tiniest hesitation? "Douglas Channon. He's the man who owns the Prince of Wales Hotel here, plus several others . . . about a dozen altogether."

"That's Merle Channon's father?" Lee tried hard to keep her tone neutral.

"Right. They live farther down the coast, about forty miles south of here. Since her mother's death Merle has acted as her father's hostess, a role that she plays to perfection."

Lee felt an overwhelming sense of despair. "You sell furniture to Mr. Channon, I take it?"

"In a big way. The Channon Hotels absorb quite a percentage of Talbot Woodcraft's output. So you see why I can't afford to upset him."

Every word Jake uttered served to deepen her sense of depression. Adopting a mask of casual amusement, she said flippantly, "I haven't met the father, of course, but from what I saw of Merle in the boutique, I can't imagine you find it a chore keeping company with *her.*"

Something in her voice must have gotten through to Jake, revealing her resentment. He slanted her a thoughtful glance, then said, "I suppose you saw Merle with me in my car on Monday night?"

Lee's senses reeled under this cruel hammerblow. A woman, *some* woman, yes, she'd accepted as much. But that particular woman, Merle Channon . . . that striking, aloof beauty with long, shining hair. Jake loved a woman's hair to be long and flowing free, Lee remembered with a stab of pain. She could picture his fingers tangling into that gorgeous black mane, his lips caressing it with passionate reverence.

Jake was looking at her, waiting for an answer to his question. Well, she wasn't going to respond in a way that would betray the agony of jealousy she felt. Taking a deep breath, she said on a light note, "Did you have someone with you that night? I didn't happen to notice." Then, jocularly, she added, "I was rather . . . occupied at the time, if you remember."

Jake's face darkened as he stared ahead at the billowing sails. "Lee, be straight with me. What is there between you and Ashley Hammond?"

"Suppose I ask in return what Merle Channon is to you?" she parried with a brittle little laugh.

"Merle and I—" he began, then stopped abruptly. "That's beside the point."

"Ditto," she said succinctly, and pulled away from him.

"You mean, your relationship with Ashley Hammond is none of my business?"

"You've got it."

"And your relationship with me . . . that's none of *his* business?"

"You catch on fast, Jake. Ten out of ten."

Jake turned his head away so that she couldn't see the expression on his face. After a brief, tense silence, he rasped, "How many others?"

"Come again?"

"Men in your life," he clipped.

She wanted to tell him that there weren't any others, not in the way he meant, not even Ashley. But pride restrained her. "Let's change the subject," she muttered.

"As you wish," Jake said indifferently. But after that he was moodily silent, and for the rest of the trip they hardly exchanged more than a few words.

Back on dry land, Jake drove the short distance to the Prince of Wales Hotel. As Lee was about to get out, he reached across and caught her hand. "Lee, about Monday evening. We'll go somewhere for dinner, and then back to my flat—okay?"

His touch seemed to scorch her skin and she pulled her hand away. "No, Jake," she said firmly.

"Give me one good reason why not," he demanded, his dark eyes searching her face.

"I can give you several. One, I'll be too busy. Two, I don't happen to want to. Three, I'm not prepared to jump each time you snap your fingers."

"Lee, this is stupid of you. . . ."

"So I'm stupid. Thanks a bunch."

"For heaven's sake!" Jake took a deep breath, and began again in a gentler tone. "Don't you see, being like this you're cutting off your nose to spite your face. You're just as keen to see me again on Monday as I am to see you. And before you start denying that, think back. On the boat today, Lee, we both entered the gates of paradise. And we could again, sweetheart, any time we want. But you stubbornly say no, because of some crazy jealousy over Merle Channon."

"It's you who's crazy," Lee jerked out furiously, "if you seriously imagine that I'm jealous about another woman." She dragged open the car door and stepped out. "Have a nice weekend, Jake. I don't doubt that you will."

"Please, Lee," he called in protest. "Won't you?"

"You're blocking the hotel forecourt," she pointed out, "so you'd better get moving. Good-bye."

"Look, we'll talk again on Monday, and . . ."

But Lee was already walking away, up the steps and into the hotel lobby. In a daze she made her way upstairs to her room, and closed the door behind her with a sigh of thankfulness. By an effort of will she had kept her poise until she was safely alone, but now her courage cracked. She had an urge to fling herself on the bed and give way to a storm of weeping. Her fate was to have fallen in love with a man who could not return her love. To Jake there was no such thing as love in the way she understood it . . . just passion, just a grabbing of whatever chances presented themselves. Lee Jordan, Merle Channon, whomever . . . what did it matter to him as long as the woman was sexy and responsive, becoming weak and pliant in his experienced hands and giving him another ego trip? Perhaps, she thought with a new stab of pain, Jake was fully aware that she was in love with him. Perhaps that had been the purpose of those long, lingering hours of bliss, the ecstasy he'd brought her with his skillful caresses . . . all to make her fall in love with him. He would become intoxicated by his sensual power over her, and then he would drop her when it suited him and seek another willing victim. Jake fondly imagined that he still hadn't quite finished with her. But he had, she vowed fiercely. There would be no more passionate interludes between them. Not on Monday, not on Tuesday, not on any day next week. Nor ever again . . .

The bedside phone rang sharply. Brushing away her foolish tears, Lee stared at it in dread. Was it Jake, returning to torment her further? If she didn't answer, she thought dismally, he'd probably be persistent and have her paged. Better to answer at once and tell him crisply to get lost.

"Yes?" she demanded in a brusque voice. "What now?"

But it wasn't Jake. "Hello, Lee. It's me . . . Ashley. I've tried to get you several times today."

"Oh, I was out. What is it, Ashley? Is something wrong?"

"No, nothing. I was just ringing to see how you're getting on."

"Oh, fine . . . just fine." She knew that her voice was still edgy, but she couldn't seem to soften it.

"No problems?"

"None at all. The staff at Talbot Woodcraft have all been most cooperative, and I don't foresee any snags we can't iron out."

"That's great." Then, after a pause, he went on, "I've been thinking so much about you . . . about us—on a personal level, I mean. It was such a pity that you had a headache on Monday evening. I had a feeling that you and I were—"

"Listen, Ashley, I've got a bath running," she lied desperately. "Must go. I'll see you at the end of the week . . . tell you everything then."

"Lee, you sound a bit upset," he said anxiously.

"Whatever gives you that idea?" Her voice was high-pitched now, veering toward a note of hysteria.

"Well . . . the way you're talking. Why don't you go and turn off the water, my dear, and come back to the phone?"

"No, I . . . I can't do that. I'm in a hurry. Good-bye, Ashley."

She hung up before he could get in another word. Would he try again? she wondered. If so, she would let the phone ring unanswered. In fact, it would be a good idea to instruct the hotel switchboard not to put through any more calls.

"I don't want to be disturbed," she told the operator. "Oh, and could you have something sent up to my room? A few sandwiches and coffee."

"What kind of sandwiches, madam?"

"It doesn't really matter . . . ham, cheese, whatever's going." Even if she got around to eating them, she wouldn't notice or care what the filling was.

Later, she stood at her window looking out. Beneath the lights on the wide esplanade, a few lovers strolled with arms entwined. While she watched, one pair stopped to exchange a long, passionate kiss. Lee turned her eyes away and looked out across the expanse of moon-silvered sea. An empty eternity.

5

~~~~~~~~~~

The morning sun, rising over the mountains, mocked Lee's mood of desolation. The day—it was Sunday—would be a lonely, dragging time for her. To make it bearable she would have to submerge herself in work.

Before breakfast she took a stroll along the esplanade. Unlike her mind, which was in torment, her body seemed to be suffused with a golden languor, rippled through with lovely echoes of ecstasy. Yesterday's long, passion-drenched hours with Jake had been followed by a night in which he had returned to haunt her dreams. And yet she knew that if he were with her now, this minute, just the lightest touch of his fingertips would arouse her once more to intense desire for him.

Lee shook her head, trying to cast out the treacherous thought. She had made her decision about Jake, and she must stick to it. Yesterday could be filed away in her memory. It had happened; it was good. She wasn't going to torture herself with remorse. When next she faced Jake, around the factory or even alone together in his office, it would be with a mask of composure. From now on their relationship would be strictly professional . . . architect and client. There was no need for any bad feeling between them; they would be adult about the whole thing.

Resolutely, she walked back to the hotel and had coffee and cereal in the sunny breakfast annex. Then, upstairs in her room, she opened her black monogrammed briefcase and spread out papers and rough sketches. She had run into a problem about where to relocate the finishing shop; if she could solve that in the course of the day it would be time well spent.

Around ten-thirty, her phone rang. Ashley again? she wondered with a frown. But the voice was that of a stranger. Firm, assured, softened by the trace of a Welsh lilt.

"Mrs. Jordan? This is Douglas Channon here."

"You mean—" Lee had almost said "Merle Channon's father." Quickly she substituted, "The Mr. Channon who owns this hotel?"

"That's me!" He sounded pleased. "My daughter and I have Jake Talbot staying with us this weekend, Mrs. Jordan, and he's been singing your praises."

"Really? In what way?"

"Jake says that you're a first-class architect, and that you're coming up with some brilliant ideas for the conversion of his factory. In fact, he's made me so interested that I'd very much like to have a talk with you."

"What about, Mr. Channon?" she asked cautiously.

"Some development plans for my place here. Nantlys Court. Are you interested, Mrs. Jordan?"

"Certainly." Lee kept her voice carefully neutral. "I'm always ready to listen to a business proposition, Mr. Channon. Whether or not it's the sort of thing my partner and I could undertake would depend, of course."

"Right, then. Why not come over here to see me, and we can look around together? Come for lunch."

"Thank you. Which day do you suggest?"

"I meant today."

"Today?" she gasped.

He chuckled. "No time like the present, I always say. Call a taxi if you haven't a car, and tell them to charge it to my account. I'll expect you when you get here, Mrs. Jordan."

"Oh, but . . ." She listened; she was talking into a dead phone. Replacing the receiver, Lee reflected ruefully that Douglas Channon was a forceful man, accustomed to getting his own way . . . a trait of character he seemed to have passed on to his daughter. She felt like calling him back to say no way could she be summoned to his presence, just like that. But then she paused, remembering what he'd said about Jake singing her praises. Had Jake engineered this whole thing, in fact, just to get her to Nantlys Court today? Yes, that must be it.

Suddenly filled with excitement, Lee deliberated over exactly what to wear, and finally decided on a slimline skirt and matching blazer of a pale coffee color, teamed with a lettuce green silk blouse. It was only after she was dressed and ready that Lee realized she didn't know how to get to Nantlys Court, beyond the fact that Jake had mentioned it lay south, on the coast. Going downstairs, she asked the desk clerk for directions, explaining, "Mr. Channon has invited me there for lunch."

The young man looked at her with a new respect, and hastily produced a large-scale folding map. Spreading it on the desk, he showed her the route. "Would you like to borrow this, Mrs. Jordan?"

"Thanks."

He folded the large sheet, and handed it to her. "Have a nice trip."

The road Lee followed out of the town turned and twisted along the rugged coastline. The sea in the sunlight was glass smooth, gently lapping the beaches of golden sand that stretched between each headland. Frequently, she came to thickly wooded glens through which ran crystal-bright streams rushing down from the mountains that loomed to her left, majestic rolling slopes carpeted in soft shades of green and the purple-brown of autumn heather.

At a point where the public road turned inland, a driveway was signposted Nantlys Court. For a while it curved downward between oak and sycamore trees, constantly bridging a stream that she guessed was seething with trout. After a few hundred yards the trees thinned out and she obtained her first view of the house poised on its knoll against the skyline. Impressed, fascinated, she stopped the car and gazed at this architectural extravaganza, a gloriously eccentric Moorish temple which nonetheless fitted perfectly into its setting on the rugged Welsh coastline. Two squat circular towers in rose-tinged stonework, enriched and embellished with intricate decorative features, flanked the house's main wing. This three-tiered structure was coolly colonnaded and topped with an oriental dome and delicate minarets that seemed to float against the sky. As a setting, rolling lawns studded with exotic shrubs and small trees stretched to an ornamental lake, where Lee could see a group of gliding white swans. Development plans, Douglas Channon had said on the phone. What kind of development plans? she wondered with a faint twinge of anxiety. This building surely was perfect just as it was. Not the sort of place where she herself would ever wish to live, but its very existence somehow added to life's richness.

Thoughtfully, she drove on, then pulled up on the wide sweep of smooth gravel before the main entrance.

A white-jacketed manservant appeared from within, and came hurrying down the steps to meet her.

"Mrs. Jordan?"

"That's right."

"Mr. Channon told me to keep a lookout for you. Will you come this way, please?"

Lee was led to a sunny patio where the weekend party was gathered for prelunch drinks. Her eyes immediately found Jake, who was perched on a decorative stone balustrade that overlooked the grounds. His back was to her and he didn't turn around.

A tall man with iron-gray hair at once broke away from his companions and came forward to greet her. He was elegantly clad in pale, knife-creased slacks and a navy-blue blazer with silver buttons, a red silk paisley scarf tied loosely at the throat. Obviously, Lee thought, Merle had inherited her looks and flair from her father, as well as her forceful character.

"Welcome to Nantlys Court, Mrs. Jordan. It's so kind of you to come at such short notice." Douglas Channon's smile was warm and his handshake firm. "Now, let's fix you up with a drink, and I'll introduce you to the others. This is my daughter Merle. Mrs. Jordan is the architect who's come to advise Jake about his factory conversion, Merle."

As they nodded to one another, Lee caught a flash of venom in the green-gold eyes, but all her attention was fixed on Jake, beyond Merle. Hearing Lee's name, he'd spun around quickly. He looked stunned, she realized, and by no means pleased.

Douglas Channon chuckled. "It's no use you frowning like that, my dear fellow. You can't expect to have exclusive rights to this clever young woman for Talbot Industries. I daresay you're sorry now that you went on so enthusiastically about her abilities, eh? But she's going to do some work for me, too, aren't you, my dear?"

"Well, I don't know about that yet," Lee murmured, dismayed at Jake's reaction. What a fool she'd been to imagine that he'd engineered her invitation to Nantlys Court. Far from wanting her here, he seemed very hostile.

"Wise woman to be cautious," observed Douglas Channon, who was clearly enjoying Jake's surprise. "But I'm quite sure that you'll like what I'm going to propose, Mrs. Jordan. All that can wait until after lunch, though."

In a daze, Lee shook hands with the other guests . . . the local member of Parliament and his wife, the chairman of the district council and a statuesque opera soprano he was apparently trying to persuade to make a guest appearance at the regional Eisteddfod next year. Plus a few others Lee was scarcely aware of, her attention being focused on Jake. He was standing with Merle by the balustrade, his dark eyes moodily following her progress.

A few minutes later, while Lee was trying hard to keep up a flow of pleasantries with a paunchy, earnest little man who was the manager of one of Douglas Channon's hotels, a hand touched her elbow from behind. The pressure of Jake's fingers was unmistakable, and an electric shock jolted her arm, nearly making her spill her drink.

"Hello, Lee." His tone was cool, anger barely concealed.

"Hi, Jake!" She turned and gave him a bright, false smile.

Drawing her to one side, he demanded harshly, "Why have you come here?"

"Because I was invited by Mr. Channon." She managed to keep her voice light, fighting against the waves of pain that made her feel faint.

"You needn't have accepted the invitation."

"Why not? I wasn't doing anything today."

"You could have invented an excuse, for heaven's sake."

Nothing now would make her admit that she'd come in the expectation that it was what Jake himself wanted. She said frostily, "Why should I pass up a promising business proposal just because I knew that *you* would be here?"

"Surely you realized that it would be an awkward situation?"

Lee felt the sting of hot tears, and was furious with herself. "Don't worry," she said, trying to hide a choke in her voice. "I won't cramp your style with Merle."

Jake's face darkened. "There's no need to be like that, Lee."

"Isn't there? I'd have thought there was every reason. But that just shows what different kinds of people we are, doesn't it?"

Merle came over to them, moving slinkily. In hip-hugging sharkskin jeans and a scarlet top that was tied to leave her midriff bare, she exuded a breath-robbing sexuality. She linked the fingers of both hands possessively around Jake's arm. Her smiling green-gold eyes held a sneer for Lee.

"Daddy seems to think you're a real find. But don't let him push you around, Lee. If you think his proposition is more than you're competent to handle, you needn't be afraid of saying no. I'll back you up, if he tries to pressure you."

"Thank you, Merle, but I'm quite able to speak up for myself."

Merle shrugged, and said, "Jake darling, let's forget the tennis doubles this afternoon. Playing against Ian and Cynthia Warner is so tame. I'd much rather we spent the afternoon by the pool."

"But won't the Warners feel let down?"

Merle waved aside that objection. "They'll easily find

someone else to give them a game. So it's the pool then, darling?"

Still Jake hesitated, glancing uneasily at Lee. "How about you? I daresay Merle could fix you up with a swimsuit."

"But she'll be fully occupied with Daddy in architectural chat. Won't you, Lee?"

"That's right," Lee agreed hastily, trying to adopt a tone of enthusiasm. "I came here on business, Jake, don't forget. Your father's plans sound most intriguing, Merle."

Lunch, an excellent buffet served semi-alfresco in the large, plant-filled conservatory, was a miserable affair for Lee. Merle was like a smooth, sleek cat, satiated with cream, and she scarcely spared Lee a glance. Over coffee, before the party broke up for the afternoon's varied activities, Lee found Jake at her side.

"We've got to talk," he muttered. "I'll see you later, when you're through with Douglas."

"What's there to talk about?" she demanded coolly. "Our reasons for being at Nantlys Court have nothing to do with each other."

He gave an impatient exclamation. "You're being silly, Lee. It would have been much better all 'round if you'd not come here today."

"Fortunately," she said crisply, "I don't have to pay heed to what you think I should or shouldn't do. Ah, here's Mr. Channon coming over. Good-bye, Jake."

He put a hand on her arm as she turned away. "Listen . . . come and find me when you're through. We . . . we can stroll down to the beach or something before you leave."

"Won't Merle object?" she said sarcastically.

"For pity's sake, just do as I say."

Douglas Channon's arrival prevented her from answering him. "Ready for the off, Mrs. Jordan?" he asked with a warm, winning smile that was meant to convey that she now had his undivided attention.

"Sure, Mr. Channon. And very intrigued, I might add."

The older man winked at Jake as he laid a hand on her arm and drew her away. "This is confidential, between architect and client. So you can make yourself scarce, my friend."

Jake hesitated, meeting Lee's eyes in a look of appeal. She gave him no encouragement and, abruptly, he turned on his heel and strode off. Douglas Channon led Lee through to the main entrance hall of the house, which was a grand chamber with a lofty ceiling formed of interlocking arches. Sunlight flooded in through three long windows, bringing to vivid life the tessellated floor. The walls were decorated with complicated geometric patterns in the Moorish style.

"Jake is a darned fine businessman," Douglas commented. "But he's a poor loser."

"I don't follow, Mr. Channon."

He chuckled. "You will, my dear Lee. You see, I believe in playing my hunches, and I have a very definite hunch that you're quite the best woman to come my way in a long time."

Lee gave him a cool, straight look, to establish once and for all that his plans for her had better be restricted to architectural matters. Then, smiling, she said in an affable voice, "On the phone you said you wanted my professional advice, Mr. Channon."

He nodded briskly, not betraying that he'd got the message—but she knew he had. "Let me fill you in. I bought this place nine years ago when I first began to be really successful. I suppose, to be quite frank, it was meant as an outward symbol of my success . . . a touch of vainglory, if you like."

"I don't blame you," said Lee. "It must be really

something to own such a fabulous house. Everything about it is so right . . . the style, the magnificent setting. Yet who would ever have thought that the Moorish manner would fit so harmoniously into a Welsh background. It does, though. The original architect must have been a man of vision. A real genius."

Douglas Channon's gray eyes kindled with pleasure. "I'm so glad you like it. And what Nantlys Court needs now is for another genius to come along and transform it."

"Into what?"

"That's for you to say. The point is, the place is too big for me now. It was different when my wife was alive. She loved it here, and enjoyed entertaining. Merle's very good at acting hostess for me, but she's restless, and how long she'll—" He broke off, then added with a smile, "I suppose I could also claim that I'm too big for Nantlys Court these days, in the sense that I no longer need such a flamboyant home as indication of my worth."

Lee found herself rather liking him for his straightforwardness and candor. "You're thinking of turning it into a hotel?"

He shrugged. "Or whatever. I want to pick your brains, my dear Lee. The days when a place like this could be a private home are really over. It's ideal for entertaining, of course, but without guests here it's a bit like a mausoleum. Much too big. So how do you see the future of Nantlys Court? It could be opened to the public as a sort of stately home, I suppose. But it's somewhat isolated for that. The same objection of isolation would apply to a museum, or even a nursing home. Come, let's stroll around and see what strikes you."

It really was a fabulous place, Lee discovered. Downstairs was a succession of elegant rooms . . . a salon done over in plushy velvet, a glittering white-and-gold ballroom, ornate dining room and lofty chambers for music and billiards. Upstairs, the dozen or so bedrooms were huge and splendid, fitted now with every modern convenience, including large *en suite* bathrooms. Everything was in immaculate condition.

"You must have spent a fortune getting it up to this standard of luxury," Lee observed.

"You can say that again!"

"Then . . . frankly, Mr. Channon, in my opinion it would be crazy to think of redesigning the whole interior for a totally new purpose. Nantlys Court is perfect just as it is. To turn it into a hotel would involve dividing up these gorgeous bedrooms, making two or three out of one and spoiling the original proportions. On the other hand . . ."

"Yes?" he asked eagerly.

"You said that it's ideal for entertaining, and I agree. The way I see it, with a minimum of alteration, you could turn Nantlys Court into a sort of super-luxury retreat for high-level business conferences—leasing the place out to corporations who wouldn't care how much they had to pay to get unique accommodations like these. Total seclusion guaranteed, in luxurious and beautiful surroundings. A master chef in the kitchens, superb service provided and every facility for leisure activities—swimming, tennis, golf, horseback riding, perhaps. Whatever."

Douglas Channon answered her with an exclamation of delight. "Brilliant, my dear Lee."

"Not all that brilliant," she said, grinning ruefully. "I guess I've just talked myself out of a lucrative conversion job. There'd be so little to be done, architecturally."

"You've just talked yourself into something much better," he told her. "I said I'm a man who plays his hunches, and what's coming over to me loud and clear right now is that you could be a big asset to me. So how about signing on as architectural consultant to Channon Hotels, on a nice fat retainer?"

"But . . ."

"Think about it, Lee. No strings—just a straightforward business proposition."

They were standing by the window of one of the tower bedrooms, overlooking the rolling green acres of the nine-hole golf course. On a terrace just below them was the swimming pool, and stretched out on lounge chairs beside the glittering blue water were several figures, including Merle and Jake. Lee watched as Merle, wearing a minuscule bikini that revealed every luscious curve of her splendid body, leaned across and playfully ran a questing finger down the muscled length of Jake's chest, from the base of his throat to the top of his black hipster briefs. Jake's hand came up and caught hers and he turned to her swiftly, no doubt grinning into her eyes.

Sickened, Lee swung away from the window. "I'm sorry, Mr. Channon, but I couldn't accept the job," she said abruptly. "Though I'm flattered you offered it to me, of course."

He looked surprised. "It's quite an opportunity for an architect, you know. I'm adding new hotels to my chain at the rate of two or three each year."

"I realize that. But . . . well, I have a partner and we operate from Bristol. I . . . I just don't feel that it would work out."

"Think about it," he said again. "There's no rush. The offer remains open. Now, much as I'd like to stay chatting with you, I suppose I should pay some attention to my other guests. And I expect you'd like to join the young people at the pool?"

"No!" she exclaimed, too fiercely. "I . . . I'm sorry, Mr. Channon, but I really ought to get going right away. I've so much work on hand."

"On a Sunday?"

"Don't tell me that *you* never work on Sundays," she parried.

He smiled ruefully. "But then I'm getting to the age when I have nothing else in my life but my work."

Douglas Channon insisted on walking with Lee to her car, and she was thankful to escape without catching another glimpse of Jake.

As Lee drove back to Aberdyffryn on the winding, hilly road, she blazed with mortification at the memory of Jake and Merle by the pool. The intimacy of Merle's sensuous caress had been blatant, designed to indicate total possession. Had the wretched woman spotted Lee with her father at the upstairs window, and made the move deliberately at that moment to demonstrate that Jake belonged to her? It made no difference, either way. The point was that she had seen Jake accept her caress as a promise, no doubt, of something much more intimate in the coming night.

Back at the hotel, Lee marched straight across the foyer, collected her key at the desk and went up to her room. For a few moments she sat on the bed, getting herself together, wondering bleakly if she could stick out her stint at Talbot Industries. A tap at the door interrupted her spinning thoughts, and she automatically called "Come in," imagining that it must be one of the hotel staff.

To her astonishment, it was Ashley who entered. Lee was so taken aback that she just sat and stared at him in stunned silence.

"Hello, Lee," he greeted her with an uncertain smile. "They told me that you'd just arrived back. You don't seem very glad to see me, my dear."

"But . . . when? Why?" she floundered.

"I got here just before lunch," he explained. "You sounded so strange on the phone last night, as if you were very upset about something. I was worried, so I thought I'd drive over to see you. They told me at the desk that you'd gone out to lunch, so I ate alone and then hung around hoping you'd be back before I had to leave."

Lee stood up, running her fingertips through her silky hair to ease it at the temples. She felt oddly touched by Ashley's concern for her, but wished to goodness he hadn't taken it into his head to spring this surprise visit.

"I'm sorry you had such a long wait, Ashley. But I'm fine, honestly I am."

Ashley came over to her and placed a hand on each of her shoulders, studying her face intently. "You don't *look* fine, my dear. Anything but." He hesitated. "Who were you lunching with? Jake Talbot?"

"What makes you think that?" she asked, startled.

"I thought perhaps you'd taken up my suggestion of going to see that mountain cottage of his."

"No, of course not!" Then, lamely, she added, "Actually, I was lunching at the home of the man who owns this hotel."

"Really? What was that all about?"

"Oh, just that he has this huge mansion, a few miles along the coast, that's too big for him now as a home, and he's thinking of converting it to another use. He wanted to pick my brains . . . his own words."

"I hope you told him that picking your brains doesn't come cheap, Lee. Sounds to me like he was trying to get valuable advice for free."

"No, nothing like that." She wasn't going to refer to Jake's part in all this; she felt far too vulnerable to talk about Jake without revealing her splintered emotions. Neither was she going to mention the advisory job Douglas Channon had offered her . . . the job it was unthinkable that she could accept. The sooner she could free herself from this area of West Wales, free herself of Jake and Merle, the better it would suit her. "I'm quite sure Mr. Channon would willingly have commissioned us, but in honesty I had to tell him that the place was best left well alone. I suggested he could turn it into a super-luxury conference house with the absolute minimum of alteration."

Ashley laughed. "And thereby talked Hammond and Jordan out of a nice lucrative job! It's lucky we're not short of work, or I might think you'd mishandled the situation. Hey, Lee, it's nothing to look so depressed about, losing a possible commission. You win some, you lose some, in this game. Tell you what, let's go for a drive and find somewhere pleasant to have dinner. How about it?"

She started to say no, pleading tiredness, then changed her mind. Ashley had been concerned about her, and had driven all this way to try and cheer her up. He was her business partner, and a valued friend besides, so she could hardly just send him packing.

"Sounds great!" she said, forcing a smile. "Give me a couple of minutes to freshen up. I'll join you downstairs."

They drove northward out of the town, the road climbing steadily until they had a wide panoramic view of sea and coastline. In the westering sun the great stretch of water was like hammered gold, and the sky was a canopy of vivid color.

Ashley wanted to know what progress she'd made during the week, and Lee outlined her ideas about the extensions to Talbot Woodcraft. He listened intently, occasionally putting in a question or comment. Then Lee suddenly found herself saying something that hadn't even surfaced in her thoughts before.

"If our outline proposals are accepted, Ashley, I'd rather someone else took on the detailed work. I . . . I mean, I'd still supervise, but I don't want to spend a lot of time rushing back and forth between Bristol and Aberdyffryn."

"Don't you like the place?" he asked.

"It's a nice little town, of course, but . . ."

"You find it a bit lonely here, I daresay," Ashley suggested, and his voice had a cheerful overtone. "Well, there's really no reason why you should make more than the occasional trip, if we put someone competent on the job. Young Martin, for instance. I can't say I relish the thought of you being away a lot, just when . . ." He glanced at her with a smile, allowing his unsaid words to convey their meaning.

With dismay Lee realized that her impetuous remark, intended to get her out of one difficult situation, was landing her right in another. Ashley would feel encouraged to pursue her now with even greater determination. How could she find a way of turning him down without being unkind about it?

They stopped for dinner at a small wayside inn with whitewashed walls, and sat in the slowly deepening dusk at a rustic table in the pretty garden. The food was very good—broiled Welsh lamb cutlets accompanied by homegrown vegetables. With this, they drank a glass of locally brewed ale.

"Not too primitive a place for you, I hope?" Ashley queried anxiously.

"Not a bit. It's charming."

"I like it, too, for a change." There was a tender look in his quiet gray eyes. "It's good for us to get away from work worries now and then, Lee. You look very lovely, my dear, and the fresh air has brought the color back to your cheeks. I felt concerned earlier, when I found you looking so pale and wan."

"I guess I really did need a break like this," she murmured, with a little shrug.

"Then I'm infinitely glad I came today." Ashley's brows knitted in a frown. "I was in two minds before I set out, you know, wondering if you'd welcome me."

"What a thing to think." She laughed reprovingly, then seized on a chance to divert the conversation. "Do look at that kitten, trying to wash its face like a grownup cat. Isn't it sweet?"

Ashley smiled distractedly. The silence between them lengthened, then he began in a low voice, "It's over eighteen months now since Stephen's death. That's quite a long time, Lee . . . too long, some would think."

"Too long?" she queried, her heart sinking at what lay before her.

"It was a terrible shock for you, I know . . . especially with all those unsavory details coming out at the inquest. But you mustn't let the unhappy past stand in the way of making a new life for yourself . . . finding happiness again."

"But I *am* happy," she protested. "My work gives me a lot of satisfaction. I have a very good life."

"That's true, of course, to a degree," he granted. "I really admire you for the way you coped at that traumatic time, the way you threw yourself into the partnership. You've proved yourself beyond all my hopes and expectations, and you've won respect all around. It must be very rewarding for you to have achieved such status in the profession, I realize that. But there are other things a woman needs in her life, my dear, a different kind of happiness."

"Please believe me, Ashley . . . I'm not looking for any other kind of happiness."

He gave a deep sigh and began again. "I can understand how you must have felt after Stephen's death . . . that you could never put your trust in a man again. But we're not all cast in the same mold, you know."

"I'm aware of that," she said with a gentle smile. "You, for instance, are one of the most straightforward and honest people I've ever met, Ashley. Having you as my partner, and my close friend, has always meant a great deal to me—and it always will." How shameful, Lee thought unhappily, that when someone as kind and decent as Ashley was working 'round to a proposal of marriage, her thoughts were still centered on a man who was nothing but a sexual opportunist. If she had any sense at all, she would be encouraging Ashley, making an easy opening for him. Instead, she was doing everything she could to head him off.

"Darling Lee," he said hesitantly, "you don't seem to understand . . . I want us to be more than close friends. I'm asking you to marry me."

She shook her head sadly. "No, Ashley. I'm immensely flattered, but . . . it's out of the question."

He looked distressed. "I've been clumsy, I've tried to rush you. Don't give me an answer immediately, my dear. Take all the time you want."

"My answer will always be the same," Lee told him. "I'm sorry, Ashley, truly I am, but I'd prefer our relationship to continue just the way it is."

Diffidently, he reached out and touched her hand, as if afraid she would snatch it away angrily. "I'll go on hoping that you'll change your mind, my sweet girl."

"I wish you wouldn't, honestly."

He smiled at her wistfully, then got to his feet, offering her a hand up. "I suppose we'd better be wending our way back."

"Please, Ashley, you must try to accept that there can't be . . ."

"I'm not listening, darling," he broke in quickly. "I can be stubborn when I want something very much."

6

Lee had scheduled to spend Monday morning going through her proposals for the new work-flow layout with the works manager, Dylan Lambert, to check that nothing had been overlooked. They were in the veneering department when, at around ten o'clock, she heard the sound of a familiar car engine. Glancing through a window, she saw Jake's white Mercedes drawing into the courtyard. He'd presumably driven straight from Nantlys Court this morning.

"I . . . I'm sorry, Dylan, what was that you were saying?" she asked apologetically.

He gave her a faintly puzzled look. "It's about these benches, Lee. We don't really have enough space to handle the throughput properly. The men keep falling over themselves all the time."

"Yes, of course." She tried to give her hundred percent attention to the problem, with scant success. Her thoughts kept turning to Jake. Would she encounter him today around the factory? Or . . . might he summon her to his office again? And if so, what then? How should she act toward him now? She could be briskly businesslike, making it clear that their personal relationship was over and done with. Of course, she had to be prepared for the possibility that Jake, having returned to Merle's willing arms over the weekend, might choose to ignore the fact that there'd ever been anything between him and Lee Jordan. If so, that was just fine with her, she thought defiantly.

Noon came and went, still with no sign or sight of him. And then, at about twelve-thirty, she was called to the phone with the words, "The boss wants to speak to you, Mrs. Jordan."

Her heart was hammering wildly as she picked up the receiver, but she managed a cool, "Hello."

"Lee, what the hell did you think you were doing yesterday, shooting off like that without a word?"

"It was Mr. Channon I went to Nantlys Court to see," she pointed out. "There was no reason for me to hang around once I'd finished my business with him."

"And that's another thing," Jake charged in accusingly. "Just what's he up to? He was very cagey when I tackled him."

"If you really want to know," she said, marveling at the coolness in her voice, "he asked my advice about a possible development plan. I gave it, and that was that. Finished. And now if you don't mind, Jake, I'd like to get back to work."

"No," he said brusquely. "You and I have got to talk, Lee. We'll go out and have some lunch."

"I . . . I can't."

"Why not? Have you another lunch date?"

"No, but I'm far too busy to—"

"Since you're working on a project for me," Jake interrupted, "I'm the one to decide how you allocate your time. So . . . I'll meet you in the courtyard in fifteen minutes. Okay?"

"There's just no point," Lee insisted, her heart thudding painfully. "You and I haven't anything to talk about."

"I say we have, darn you!" As long as Jake was browbeating her, she was able to hold out against him. But then his tone changed and he added in a soft, coaxing voice, "Please, Lee . . . it's surely not much to ask. I'll take you to a place on the edge of town where they do extremely good seafood. You'll like it, I promise."

"Okay, then," she said weakly. Perhaps, she reasoned with herself, a lunch date was a good idea after all. It might serve to clear the air between them.

"Fine. See you, Lee."

Jake was there before her, waiting by his car. As he held open the door and helped her get in, his fingers lightly caressing her shoulder, Lee couldn't help shivering. Sitting beside him on the short drive, she was dismayed to find that Jake's sensual magnetism completely undermined her determination to be coolly professional toward him. He was wearing a sports jacket today, in a fine pale green wool with a small check design in brown and black. His shirt was an ochre yellow, and at the edge of the cuff where tiny dark hairs curled she could see the broad gold band of his wristwatch. In fascination she watched his hand on the gearshift . . . the long, sensitive fingers that had caressed her, bringing her such exquisite delight. Lee swallowed hard; she was insane ever to have agreed to such a meeting.

The Three Lobsters was on the edge of town, halfway up a hill. Leaving the car, they made their way through a leafy garden to a pleasant stone-built house with pointed gables and fretted chimneypots. Inside, a long gallery stretched across the rear of the building, with basketwork tables and chairs and red checkered cloths. One entire wall was glass, giving a magnificent view of Aberdyffryn nestling around the bay, with glimpses of the rugged coastline stretching beyond.

They were escorted to a table by a plump, jolly-looking woman in a neat gingham apron. "Good it is to see you, Mr. Talbot," she said chattily in her lilting Welsh voice. "How are you today? The young lady, I believe, I have not had the pleasure of meeting before."

Jake introduced them. "Mrs. Lee Jordan . . . Mrs. Bronwyn Davies, who owns this restaurant—which is the best for miles around. Mrs. Jordan is an architect from Bristol, Bronwyn, who's come to work out what can be done to get Talbot Woodcraft all under one roof."

Lee received a warm glance of approval. "That's the ticket! Nice it is to hear of young women showing the menfolk that we're every bit as capable as they are."

"Unfortunately," Lee replied with a laugh, "the menfolk don't always take it so kindly."

"Mrs. Jordan," Jake observed dryly as they sat down and were handed menus, "is quite a star performer all 'round. Now, what do you specially recommend today, Bronwyn?"

"The sea bass is very good. Fresh caught this morning."

He glanced at Lee. "Let's settle for that, then, shall we?"

"I think I'll have the turbot," she said deliberately, not intending to let him make her decisions for her.

Jake cocked an eyebrow in amusement. "Are you going to let me choose the wine?"

"Thanks, but I don't want any wine."

"Oh, come on . . . just a glass. We'll have a bottle of the chablis, Bronwyn." When the woman had departed, he threw her a questioning look across the table. "You're in a very waspish mood today."

"You can cut out the snide remarks," she told him crisply.

"Because I called you waspish? You've just proved it, haven't you?"

"I was referring," she said in a deliberate tone, "to that remark you made about me to Mrs. Davies."

His lips twitched. "You object to being called a star performer? Highly flattering, I'd have thought."

"I could have done without the snide undercurrent."

His face became serious and he studied her intently for several long moments. "Lee, this is crazy. Whatever happened to that wonderful, exciting woman who spent Saturday with me?"

"Saturday," she said with a catch of breath, "was a mistake."

"All of it?"

"All of it," she said firmly.

His eyes glowed, burning into her. "Okay, if that's how you see it. So let's make a few more mistakes."

"There you go again," she burst out furiously. "You just can't resist making clever cracks."

"On the contrary, I was making a very serious suggestion." His voice was low and rich, sending flurries of excitement pulsing through her. "Please, Lee . . . with you leaving Aberdyffryn so soon, there isn't time for us to play about. We'd be mad not to grab every possible chance we have of being together."

"Which is why, I suppose, you chose to spend a lot of the weekend at Nantlys Court?" Oh damn, Lee thought wretchedly, why had she made such a stupidly revealing remark? It was playing right into his hands.

Again Jake was silent for a long, throbbing moment. Then he snapped through tight lips, "Let's leave Merle Channon out of this, Lee."

"I didn't mention Merle Channon."

"Oh, yes you did. Just as if you'd shouted her name from the rooftops."

"Listen," she said urgently, clenching her hands together beneath the checkered tablecloth, "your relationship with Merle Channon doesn't bother me one little bit."

"So what are you so uptight about?"

Mercifully, the arrival of a young waitress with their fish gave Lee a chance to get a grip on herself.

"Jake," she said, when they were alone again, "what happened between you and me . . . well, I'm not about to make a big issue out of it. . . ."

"But you should," he cut in, the look in his eyes like a soft, sensuous caress. "What happened between us was out of this world."

"It was good sex," she conceded matter-of-factly, struggling to keep her voice steady.

"Just that . . . good sex?"

"What else, for heaven's sake? If you expected to . . . to cast some sort of spell around me, so that when I go back to Bristol at the end of this week you could chalk up yet another adoring female who was eating out her heart for you . . . well, you can think again, Jake Talbot!"

He had no immediate comeback to that, which gave her another momentary respite. She looked through the window at the wide expanse of ocean, glittering silver-gilt in the noonday sun. A lone yacht was running before the wind, skimming the water gracefully.

Jake's voice held a curious expression that she couldn't interpret. "Lee, when you leave Aberdyffryn at the end of this week, it won't be the last we shall see of one another, will it? I imagine that you'll be back and forth while the work on the factory goes ahead?"

"Always assuming," she retorted, glancing back at

him, "that you accept Hammond and Jordan's outline proposals."

His smoke-brown eyes met hers. "I don't think there's any doubt on that score."

She should have been rejoicing inwardly, but instead she felt a heavy weight of depression. For the first time ever she had half wanted *not* to win a commission she'd been pitching for.

"I trust you're under no illusion," she lashed out at him, her gaze fixed on the small vase of yellow dahlias in the center of the table, "that you'd be buying me along with the building plans."

"I'm aware that you're not for sale, Lee," he replied quietly.

"I'm glad that's clear. In any case," she went on, "I won't need to come here all that often. Most of the routine supervision will be handled by one of our staff."

Jake's mouth tightened. "That wasn't part of the contract."

"We don't have a contract with you as yet," she reminded him. "But no need to worry, you won't be missing out on anything. Talbot Woodcraft's extensions will receive the same care and meticulous attention to detail that we give to every job we undertake."

"That I didn't doubt for a moment."

"So you'll have no gripe then, will you?"

There was a look of bafflement in his deepset brown eyes. He spoke in a low voice that was scarcely above a whisper. "Lee, however much or however little we manage to see of each other in the time ahead, don't let's be on hostile terms. We've proved that things can be so good between us . . . more than good!"

Lee closed her eyes against a feeling of dizziness. Jake used the phrase "good . . . more than good," when to her those hours spent with him had been an enchanted world she had never known before. "Good," he labeled their relationship, when there were no words adequate in her vocabulary to describe his lovemaking, or the emotional joy it had brought her that was something over and above the sheer physical ecstasy. One thought sprang into clear focus from the confusion of her brain: I must not let him guess that I love him. That would be to hand Jake the victory he sought and the shameful defeat she dreaded.

"I've got news for you, Jake," she said crisply, hiding her misery behind a bright, false smile. "It's not a good idea to place so much importance on something that was essentially unimportant."

"Unimportant?" he jerked out incredulously.

"That's what I said."

"My God, Lee, but you're hard."

Bronwyn Davies bustled up to their table. "Goodness me, not a single morsel of that lovely fish you've touched, the pair of you. Come now, give it back and I'll have it hotted up. I'll not allow it to be said that my customers have to eat cold food."

"I'm sorry, Mrs. Davies," Lee apologized, dismayed to realize that she'd been toying with her fork without once raising it to her mouth. "We were . . . talking."

"Talking, eh?" She chuckled. "What's wrong, my dear? Does this hardheaded businessman strike a tough bargain?"

Lee nodded, carefully avoiding Jake's eyes. "You could say that."

"Then don't let him." Bronwyn smiled as she picked up their platters and turned to head for the kitchen. "Men seem to imagine that they rule the world, and it's high time they learned different."

When she'd gone they were both silent. After a moment Jake topped Lee's wineglass and refilled his own. In a carefully neutral voice, he remarked, "Douglas Channon said that he'd asked you to stay on for a while yesterday, and join the rest of us at the pool. But you insisted that you had to get away at once."

"That's right," she agreed tightly.

"Why, after I'd made it clear I wanted to talk to you?"

On the brink of a sharp retort, Lee hesitated. She could turn Ashley's visit to good account. "Ashley drove up from Bristol," she said, hoping to convey the impression that this had been prearranged. "We went for a drive, and stopped for dinner at a delightful little rustic inn right out in the countryside. It was a really super evening."

The muscles of Jake's jaw went taut. "You surprise me," he commented scathingly. "I wouldn't have thought Ashley Hammond was the type to enjoy rustic charm."

"But then you don't really know anything about Ashley, do you?"

"Clearly not, if you find him attractive. The man must have hidden depths. Or perhaps it's simply a matter of mutual convenience? Partners in the firm, partners for life—all neat and tidy. Is that it?"

Lee gave an elaborate shrug. "No comment! You're free to form whatever conclusions you like."

"Tell me, Lee . . . is Hammond aware that you spent the day with me on Saturday?"

She refused to be discomfited. "The subject didn't happen to arise."

"You were too busy?" he suggested nastily.

"As I said, the subject didn't arise." She gave him a long, cool look. "Ashley and I do have other things to talk about, Jake. You're only one client among many."

His mouth twisted wryly. "Was that intended to cut me down to size? Don't worry, Lee, I'm not suffering from the delusion that Hammond and Jordan is in desperate need of a commission from Talbot Woodcraft. I chose your firm because, for the sort of thing I want done, it's probably one of the best there is. And, in any field, the best is likely to be in high demand."

"I'm glad you realize that."

Bronwyn Davies came hurrying back to their table bearing the reheated platters. "Now then, here we are. You'll eat this up while it's hot, even if I have to stand over you myself."

Jake gave her a brief, distracted smile. "It's good of you, Bronwyn. I'm afraid we got so bogged down in talk we just forgot your excellent food. But we'll do it justice this time, I promise."

"Well, see you do!"

Neither of them seemed to have much appetite. Lee had a struggle to consume a reasonable portion of her turbot. The tense, prickly silence between them was unnerving. Once or twice she ventured a noncontentious remark about the food, the weather, only getting a grunted monosyllable in response. When she finally laid down her fork, she glanced up to find herself confronted with the full impact of Jake's dark gaze.

"So what are we going to do, Lee?" he asked, the throbbing timbre of his voice making her skin prickle.

"Do?" she echoed, moistening dry lips. "About what?"

"About us."

"Nothing," she said on a rising, hysterical note. "I thought I'd made that clear."

Anger flared in his eyes and he shook his head irritably. "That's stupid talk! For the next few days, Lee, you're here and I'm here. Two people who are extremely attracted to each other. Two people for whom the chemistry is wonderfully right. I can feel it, and so can you."

"Speak for yourself," she retorted, trembling as the familiar ache of love and longing spread through her like a rapidly flooding tide.

"Okay, I will speak for myself. I want you, Lee. Right this minute I want you like crazy, just as I've wanted you every hour of the day and night since we met. You set me on fire, sweetheart, and the flames are burning me up."

"Too bad," she riposted, shaking herself in an attempt to fend off the insidious lure of his virile magnetism. "But I'm sure you can turn elsewhere to have those fires quenched."

"I said we won't discuss Merle Channon," he said through gritted teeth.

"Were we discussing her? Does that mean Merle Channon is the only woman you have currently available? You'd better look to your laurels, Jake."

He brushed aside her sarcasm with an angry wave of his hand. "This is crazy . . . utterly ridiculous. I need you, Lee, and you need me . . . despite the fact that you're lying in your teeth to deny it. For pity's sake, why do you have to carry on like this? It could all be so beautifully simple and uncomplicated."

"The typical male fantasy scenario," she said scornfully. "Simple and uncomplicated sex . . . with no ties, no commitments."

"Is that what you want, Lee . . . commitment?" he asked after a moment, with a strange, thoughtful look.

Again, she could have bitten off her tongue. "I want nothing from you, Jake, except your signature at the bottom of a contract. And that, I might add, is getting less and less attractive by the minute."

He reached for her hand across the table. But she foresaw his intention and quickly moved it back out of his reach.

"Lee, let me see you this evening," he asked in a low, intense voice.

"No Jake, it's all over. It's history." She released a sigh. "If you don't insist on spoiling everything, I might just be able to keep the memory of Saturday as something wonderful that happened. I'd like to be able to look back and remember you with warmth and affection."

"Forget about warmth and affection," he clipped. "It's passion we're talking about, Lee."

"I'd like to end this conversation now," she told him, with an effort at dignity.

"Okay. Just so long as you agree to see me this evening."

"No, Jake, I won't do that."

It was as if she hadn't spoken. "How about me coming to the Prince of Wales and having dinner with you there? Or anywhere else you care to name. Please, Lee."

"No!"

He looked at her with a long, caressing glance that made her body go soft and fluid. "It wouldn't take us all that long to drive to my cottage. Maybe there you'd find yourself able to relax, and . . ."

The strength of her temptation was terrifying. That lonely little cottage, lost amid the quiet of the mountains, was where it had all begun, where she had first experienced the intense joy of Jake's caresses.

"No, Jake," she said again, but she was aware that her voice lacked its former emphasis.

"We could take food with us," he hurried on persuasively. "Leaving out the fog, we could recreate last Sunday. The same meal, the same music, the same log fire, the same fantastic feeling between us."

"I said no, and I meant it."

"But don't you see, we could go back to the beginning, back to square one. We could replay that evening, Lee, and give it a different ending."

"The ending would be the same," she insisted.

"If you're so sure of that," he demanded in soft challenge, "why are you so afraid to come to the cottage?"

Lee stared back at him, sunk in a great trough of

misery. If only she didn't love the man, she thought desperately. If only she could cure herself of the constant ache of longing to be held in his arms, to feel his hard, lean body throbbing against hers, to experience again the wild excitement of his kisses.

"Please," she begged, drained of the ability to argue with him anymore. "Just leave me alone to finish the work I came here to do. It's not much to ask."

"It's far too much," Jake said, his eyes slowly traveling over her face, lingering on her mouth before coming back to hold her gaze again.

Lee blinked back a rush of tears. "Whatever you say, Jake, however much you pressure me, I shall still refuse. I'm not even going to have lunch with you again."

For long, silent, pulsing moments, Jake regarded her across the table. Then at last he said, "I'm sorry, Lee, I didn't mean to upset you. We'll leave it at that . . . for the moment."

"For good," she pleaded. "Leave it for good."

"No, I won't agree to that," he stated, with an emphasis that sent a wash of heat through her body. "I can't agree to that."

7

─◦◦◦◦◦◦◦◦◦◦◦◦◦─

Lee left dining that evening until as late as possible, fearful that she might encounter Jake in one of the hotel's public rooms. She toyed with the idea of calling room service, but pride prevented her from taking the cowardly way out.

After their lunch at the Three Lobsters, she and Jake had driven back to the factory without exchanging more than a few overpolite sentences, almost as if they were strangers. They had parted in the courtyard, and she hadn't seen him since. What his next move would be, Lee couldn't guess. She both dreaded its coming and longed for it desperately, at one and the same time. Jake was like a fever in her blood.

As she entered the ornate dining room, ablaze with glittering chandeliers and half empty at this late hour, she met the gaze of a woman sitting alone at a table in the corner. Merle Channon. Annoyed at having allowed her feelings of dismay to register on her face, Lee gave a

hasty nod of acknowledgment and followed the maître d'
toward her usual table.

"Come and join me, Lee." The voice was arresting,
with the same cool, disdainful self-assurance she'd used
when speaking to her assistant in the boutique.

Lee felt a strong urge to refuse, but on second thought
she decided to accept. It would be interesting to find out
what Merle had to say. One thing she felt quite certain
about . . . Merle Channon's invitation had not been a
spur-of-the-moment impulse; this encounter had been
planned. Merle must have been sitting at the table waiting
for her to appear. Possibly, even, her reason for being in
the hotel tonight was simply and solely because she
wanted to engineer an apparently accidental meeting.
Giving a casual shrug, Lee took the chair the waiter was
patiently holding out for her. "I must admit," she said,
"that it gets a bit dull dining on one's own."

"I gather that you gave my father some good advice,"
Merle said, with a patently false smile.

"I'm glad he thinks so," Lee returned coolly.

"Oh, he's full of praise for you, as an architect. It's the
same with Jake." She gurgled a laugh. "Like the majority
of men, Jake and my father find it astonishing when a
woman is successful in business or a profession, despite
my own example staring them in the face."

Lee made no comment. This was Merle's party, and it
was up to her to set the pace.

"Tell me, Lee, how are things going with the plans for
the factory extension?" she inquired after a moment, and
added with an apologetic little *moue*, "Jake and I had so
many other things to talk about this weekend that I'm
afraid I didn't get around to asking him what the schedule
was."

Lee fought against the stabs of jealousy that were
keener than anything she had ever known before. Pre-
tending to take Merle's interest at face value, she said

affably, "At this stage I'm just doing a preliminary survey. A feasibility study. After Jake has approved that, then detailed drawings will have to be made and all the plans submitted to the local town planning authority, who may insist on changes. It's quite a long process. With luck, the actual building work will commence sometime early next year."

"I see. And you'll be located in Aberdyffryn all that time?"

"Hardly. This is only one job among many. I'll just be putting in an appearance from time to time."

The waiter returned, and offered Lee a menu. "Go ahead," said Merle, with a wave of her hand that set the gold bracelets on her wrist jangling. "I've already ordered."

Hiding behind the large, elaborately printed card, Lee made a token appearance of studying it, but in reality she was cursing herself for having been such an idiot as to join this woman for dinner. She had to go through with the ordeal now to the bitter end. "I'll have the duck with orange sauce," she said, choosing at random.

"And to start with, madam?"

"Oh . . . the melon, I think."

Merle's next remark, when they were alone again, came as a nasty shock. "Did you enjoy the boat trip on Saturday?"

"How do you know about that?" Lee gasped, immediately thinking what a stupid thing it was to have said.

"How do you imagine I know?" Merle's green-gold eyes glinted with amusement. "Jake is so ridiculously proud of that quaint old boat of his. He can never resist the chance to show it off to people. When he pleaded with me on Friday to be allowed to arrive at our place Saturday evening instead of lunchtime, I hadn't the heart to refuse. He's just like a small boy. But then, aren't all men when it comes to their pet hobbies?"

In a daze, Lee heard someone answering Merle and it seemed incredible that the owner of that calm, level voice could be herself. "In my opinion Jake has something to be proud of in *Lancashire Lass*. She's a fine boat."

"A museum piece, really," Merle suggested, with an ironic curl of one eyebrow. "But Jake won't be keeping it much longer. He knows how I feel about such things, and he'll soon forget his passion of the moment."

The waiter returned with the starters they'd ordered. Lee was thankful she'd chosen melon, which slipped down easily past the tightness in her throat. Merle dealt elegantly with her avocado vinaigrette.

"What brings you to Aberdyffryn this evening?" Lee asked in a bright voice, after a few moments.

"Oh, you know how it is . . . if you run a business, you have to keep close tabs on your staff. I dread to think what those girls would get up to if they didn't know I'm liable to descend unannounced at any moment. That keeps them on their toes."

"Will you be driving back to Nantlys Court tonight?"

"Heavens no! I've got something much more interesting lined up for tonight right here in Aberdyffryn," she added meaningfully.

"But you were dining alone . . . until I joined you."

"Yes, that was bad luck, but business must come first. I can't grumble, I suppose, not having given advance notice of my arrival." Merle laughed softly. "Never mind . . . the disappointment will be forgotten later on."

Lee gritted her teeth against the pain. Then she said very deliberately—and her words had a bitter truth, "I shan't be sorry to get back to Bristol at the end of this week."

There was a quickening of interest in Merle's eyes, but her voice was a casual drawl. "So what's the big attraction in Bristol? That partner of yours . . . what was his name . . . Ashley something? I gather that that he bothered to come all the way to see you yesterday. He must be devoted."

Jake talking again! Lee felt trampled on, bruised and beaten. "He is rather keen," she admitted, with a light laugh, and hated herself for using Ashley like this in her verbal sparring with Merle.

Merle shrugged. "Can't be bad, can it—keeping things in the family, so to speak? Have you fixed the date yet?"

"Not actually." A lie, or not a lie—what did it matter at this stage?

"I shouldn't hang about," Merle advised. "It sounds like you're on to a good prospect there, Lee . . . may I call you Lee? Ah, here comes our dinner. No, idiot," she snapped at the waiter, "the duck is for Mrs. Jordan. I'm having salmon."

It took all Lee's courage to make reasonable inroads into the large helping of roast duck with mixed vegetables, and look as if she were unconcernedly enjoying it. She managed to keep up a cool front right through to the end of the meal, refusing any dessert but not hurrying over the coffee. Finally, to her infinite relief, the moment came when she could get away without it being an open admission of defeat.

"You must excuse me," she said with a forced smile, "but I still have some work to do tonight."

"Yes, I must be going, too," said Merle, glancing at her wristwatch. "It's been nice chatting with you, Lee. And good luck with your Ashley."

As she hurried away, Lee paused a moment at the maître d's little desk. "Make sure that you charge my dinner to my account," she instructed him.

The man looked surprised. "But Miss Channon will expect . . ."

"Never mind what Miss Channon expects," Lee said firmly. "Please do as I say." Under no circumstances, she thought as she mounted the stairs to her room, would she accept any kind of favor from Merle Channon.

On Tuesday morning, instead of going to the factory, Lee made her way on foot to the top of Uwchfoel. This was a hill affording a fine bird's eye view of Aberdyffryn, from where she could look down at the Victorian mill building that housed Talbot Woodcraft. Her purpose was to ponder how well her tentative plans for its extension would harmonize with the little town as a whole.

It was difficult to concentrate her thoughts, though. The unpleasant encounter with Merle the night before was still agonizing her mind. She tried telling herself that she'd learned nothing she didn't know already about Merle's relationship with Jake. For the hundredth time, Lee wished that she had not set eyes on Jake Talbot again after that night in his cottage. Yet despite everything, despite the pain and heartache he was causing her, she still longed for him above everyone and everything else. . . .

With an effort, she forced her mind back to the task at hand. The mill, built for a Victorian industrialist with artistic vision, had been designed exquisitely; it could have served a more exalted purpose than the manufacture of woollen cloth. Constructed solidly of stone, with fine tall windows each surmounted by a semicircular molding, the central portion of the facade columned at street level and charmingly colonnaded above, the building had all the splendid nobility of a concert hall. It was no wonder Jake was anxious that nothing should be done to detract in any way from its present appearance.

Lee had never been a copyist. She firmly believed that any architectural design of the twentieth century should utilize the special qualities of modern materials like concrete and steel as well as recent technical innovations.

But that didn't rule out a happy blending of old and new. For the extension she had worked out an effective echo of the colonnading, and now, up here at this vantage point, she half closed her eyes to gauge the finished appearance.

"Lee, I've been looking for you everywhere."

At the sound of Jake's voice, her eyes flew wide open with shock. He was clambering up the last few feet of the steep path. He came forward to the bench where she was sitting, and stood looking down at her. His gaze swept over her face questioningly.

"When you didn't turn up at the factory this morning, I was worried," he said. "I phoned the Prince of Wales, and I even phoned the town hall, to see if you'd fixed to see anyone there. Then someone told me they'd seen you walking this way. Why on earth have you come up here, Lee?"

He might almost have been an apparition, conjured up from her inmost longings. Lee stared back at him fearfully—but the fear she felt was of herself, of her own wayward emotions that even now were urging her toward Jake so compellingly that she had to fight hard not to fling herself into his arms. He looked so achingly attractive, with his dark hair riffled by the wind and the strongly carved planes and angles of his face caught by the sudden flood of bright light as the sun burst from behind a drifting cloud.

"I . . . I came up here to get an overall view of the town," she explained in a low, tense voice. She gestured at the clipboard lying on the bench beside her, to which her various plans and schedules were fastened. "Being up here helps me picture the final result I'm aiming for."

Jake looked relieved. "I thought perhaps you'd decided you couldn't face coming back."

"Oh, you needn't worry, I'll see the job through," she returned, not hiding the bitterness in her voice.

"It wasn't the job I was thinking about, Lee."

"Don't you ever give up?" she asked with a sigh. "Don't you ever take no for an answer?"

"Not when I want something as much as I want you," he said, and the caressing look in his eyes made her weak with the pull of her emotions.

Managing a careless shrug, she said, "Well, now that you've satisfied yourself where I am and what I'm doing, perhaps you'll go away and leave me to get on with my work in peace."

"But would you be in peace?" he demanded, his voice insistent. "I'm not, Lee. I'm in torment."

She gave him a frosty glare. "Why do you exaggerate so wildly? Okay, so we discovered a strong physical attraction for each other. For you, it seems, the interest is lingering rather longer than for me. Too bad! But don't pretend that it's more than a temporary frustration. I'm sure you'll easily find a replacement to deal with that problem. And there's always your regular girlfriend, Merle Channon."

His glance was venomous. "You seem to be obsessed with Merle."

"Obsessed with Merle? That's crazy. But it revolts me to see you clinging to a burnt-out relationship with her from the lowest of motives."

His eyes flared. "Meaning?"

"Pure, unadulterated personal gain. Her father is a big customer of yours, isn't he? You admitted that much to me. So where would your factory extension program be without the flow of nice, lucrative orders from him?"

Jake took a seat at the other end of the bench and crossed his long legs. Not looking at Lee, he stared down at the town which lay below them. "*Personal* gain, you said?"

"That's what I said."

"It may interest you to know that for some years now

I've been fighting a losing battle against foreign competitors. Our product is better, no question, but theirs is a darned sight cheaper. I decided in the end that I'd have to get the whole factory under one roof, reequip and generally streamline for efficiency, if we were to keep in business. Aberdyffryn is a small place, Lee, and I employ over two hundred people. That doesn't sound like a lot, maybe, but if Talbot Woodcraft went under, it would be sheer disaster for the town."

"I'm sorry," she mumbled awkwardly.

"I'm not asking for apologies, Lee, I just want you to understand. You're quite right, Douglas Channon is a valuable customer, so I go out of my way to keep him happy."

"And his daughter!"

He swung 'round to glare at her, his face a mask of fury. "I'm sick and tired of the way you keep harping on Merle. We're supposed to be talking about you and me."

"I didn't know that we're *supposed* to be talking about anything."

She saw his fists clench as he fought to control his anger. Then suddenly, unexpectedly, he slid along the bench and reached for her hand. Lee snatched it away quickly.

"I don't want to fight with you, Lee," he groaned. "I want to make love to you. You act as if that's the biggest crime on the statute book. Yet we both know—we've proved—that between us it's the most wonderful thing imaginable."

"You've doubtless had plenty of experience to judge by," she tossed back, refusing to meet his eyes. "I imagine you regard yourself as quite an expert on the subject."

She heard Jake catch his breath impatiently. "I'm a normal, healthy male of thirty-three. Would you expect me to have missed out on my fair share of experience?"

She lifted her slender shoulders. "No, but . . ."

"I don't keep on at you about the other men in your life."

"Don't you? You seem very interested in my relationship with Ashley Hammond."

"So you admit that there is a relationship with him?"

"He's my partner," she reminded him evasively.

"Don't play around with me, Lee! I want a straight answer."

"Which you aren't going to get." She was feeling a trifle more sure of herself now and met his gaze haughtily. "It's a stalemate, Jake . . . Merle and Ashley are ruled out of order as subjects for conversation."

The glint in his dark eyes was dangerous, and Lee wished she hadn't tried being pert. But then the anger seemed to drain out of him. "Okay, that suits me fine, Lee. Why not let you and me start afresh, as if we'd just recently met? By which I mean that I won't take anything for granted because of what's happened before. On those terms, I'm looking at you now and I think you're the most lovely, desirable woman I've ever seen. I want to kiss you at this moment quite desperately."

"No!" she retorted in a shrill voice.

Jake drew nearer, but still not quite touching her. "Are you afraid?"

"Why should I be afraid?"

"Not of me, certainly. Maybe of yourself?"

His eyes watchful, he inched forward until Lee could feel his warm breath fanning her cheek. She was acutely sensitive to the virility that radiated from his lean, lithe body; she could smell his clean, tangy freshness. It made her senses swirl, and she was thankful to be sitting down.

"You're talking nonsense," she managed faintly, grasping for her reserves of strength.

Slowly, insidiously, Jake continued to come closer. Lee froze to the stillness of a statue . . . until, as his mouth finally made contact with hers, she jerked in violent response. His arms went swiftly about her shoulders, encircling her with velvet firmness and pulling her to him.

"Lee . . . oh, my darling Lee," he murmured huskily against her lips. "How I've longed to hold you in my arms again. . . ." He checked himself abruptly, and drew back a little. "No, that's not fair. I said that we'd start over. So we'll pretend this is the very first time I've held you, kissed you. We're just two people who have magically found each other, and all of a sudden the world has become a wonderful place. Isn't it so for you, too?"

Weakly, she shook her head to deny it. "Jake . . . please let me go."

"If you truly want me to let you go, sweetheart, why are you clinging to me? Why are your lips so soft and warm and inviting? Why does your body tremble as I caress you?"

"You . . . you're being horribly unfair."

"I'll let you go, my darling, and I'll not come back to bother you again," he promised, "on one condition."

"What's that?" she whispered, on a slender thread of breath.

"That you reject me with the honest language of your body, not just in insincere words." His hand sliding sensuously down the curve of her back, he went on, "Show me with your lovely body that you don't want my arms around you, don't want my lips on yours."

Lee felt herself go dizzy and helpless with her burning need for him. "You . . . you know I can't, Jake," she sobbed.

"No, my darling, you can't, can you?" Jake reached up and deftly pulled out the restraining comb and pins, so that her hair tumbled free and drifted out in long, silken tresses in the breeze from the ocean. With a shuddering sigh, he buried his face in its fragrant softness. "You're so beautiful, so utterly desirable."

"Please . . ." she begged, not knowing any longer what it was she meant as passion flared through her and the blood thundered in her ears.

Jake's mouth followed a trail of sweet plunder across her face, touching each eye with gentle lips, skimming over her delicately molded cheekbones to seize and nip the lobe of her ear. She felt the exciting rasp of his chin on her throat as he nibbled tiny kisses around the line of her jaw. And finally he homed in on her eager, welcoming mouth, her lips already parted to allow their tongues to curl about each other in a total surrender to sensual pleasure. How was it possible to pretend that this was their first kiss when it brought her such delirious joy, such a sweet tingling in her breasts, such a flood of warmth through her body, such rapturous memories of the intimacies they had shared?

She felt his hand come 'round to cup a breast, and moaned afresh with her desperate, urgent need of him. His fingers had already slipped into the vee of her striped cotton blouse, about to undo the buttons, when she floated through the swirling mist of her senses to a realization that this was broad daylight, in a public place, where anyone might come along at any minute.

"No, Jake," she protested. "Not now. Not here."

"Later, then. Tonight. We'll go to my flat."

"But I didn't mean . . ."

"It's inevitable, Lee. You know that as well as I do. Neither of us can fight this."

"I . . . I must fight it."

"Why?" he demanded. "Can you give me a reason that makes any sort of sense?"

The most telling reason in all the world, she thought despairingly. I love you, and you don't love me. I can't accept your briefly flaring passion, your desire, your lust. Without his love in return for hers, the sweetness of their sexual union would have an unbearably bitter aftermath.

Impossible, though, to tell Jake the truth, so she sought for some explanation that would convince him.

Steeling herself, she said with slow, measured words, "Jake, I'd be a hypocrite to pretend that I regret what happened between us, what we shared. But now, however hard for me, it must be over. To continue would make me feel too guilty. You see, it wouldn't be fair to Ashley."

Jake pushed himself back from her violently, and gripped her shoulders with harsh fingers that squeezed her flesh. "He means nothing to you, Lee . . . not in the way I do."

"That isn't for you to say."

"It damn well is! I know you feel no real passion for Hammond, no tormenting desire as you do for me. I only had to see you two together . . . in my office, in the hotel bar. Even when you were kissing him on the esplanade, you were looking over his shoulder at me."

Flinching, she rushed on frantically, "What you and I have felt for one another, Jake, is shallow and false . . . without true meaning."

"It represents the only truth that matters," he stated vehemently. "You will come to me tonight, Lee, because you haven't the strength to stay away."

She shook her head in furious denial. "You're wrong, Jake."

"I'll fetch you from the hotel at seven," he continued in a low, threatening voice. "You'd better be ready."

"Please, Jake . . . please don't make trouble."

"Then say that you'll come."

Her resolution was ebbing away fast. It would be so easy to agree, so thrillingly easy to give herself up once more to the joy of his lovemaking. She moistened her lips, and said huskily, "I . . . I'll think it over."

"No, say yes. Promise me."

Lee finally gave way, as deep down she'd known she

must from the very beginning. "Very well, Jake, I'll come."

The fierce tension seemed to melt from his muscles as he looked at her and gave a slow, tender smile. "Oh, my darling, it will be so wonderful. Better even than before."

She closed her eyes, unable to cope with the storm of emotions raging within her. She felt a feathertouch of Jake's lips on her brow, and then a sudden pressure on her mouth again, warm and ardent, while his body, hot and hard against hers, trembled with leashed-back passion.

"Until tonight, my sweet," he whispered huskily. "It's a pact, remember."

He lingered a moment longer, holding her, then he was gone. But even then the aura of his presence remained, cocooning her with delight. When at last Lee allowed her eyelids to flutter open Jake had disappeared from sight. She leaned back against the wooden bench and gazed up into the cerulean-blue infinity. If only, she thought with a poignant sigh, tonight could last for ever and ever, and there could be no painful tomorrow.

8

~cececececece~

The day drifted by for Lee in a golden haze. Only now and then did a dark cloud of doubt gather, but each time, she swept it aside. To experience just once again the delirious joy of being in Jake's arms, sharing with him the ecstasy of wild, unrestrained passion, was her own deliberate choice. She owed fidelity to no one; she was a free agent. So, no matter how much it cost her afterwards in heartache, she would steal for herself one more night of sensual pleasure.

After this, though, no more. Tomorrow would be Wednesday, and her proposals had to be ready for presentation to Jake by Friday. With the time lost so far, she had a great deal of catching up to do. But even that daunting realization couldn't focus Lee's thoughts sufficiently for her to make much useful progress in the course of the day.

She was up in her bedroom, putting final touches to her appearance, when the desk called to say that Jake was waiting downstairs. She gave herself a last quick onceover in the long mirror of the wardrobe, and knew that she had chosen well. The dress of supple jersey silk in a sheening hue of turquoise brought out the color of her eyes and beautifully set off the honey-blond of her loose-flowing hair and the faint golden tan of her skin. Despite the wild fluttering of her heart, she felt elegant and poised in the strappy high-heeled evening sandals. Even her own super-critical gaze told her she looked attractive. Desirable. With delicate fingertips she adjusted the scooped neckline of the dress along the swell of her breasts, then, reaching for the small phial of French perfume, she applied a few drops to her pulse points—at the temples, behind each ear, at the bend of her elbows and the inside of her wrists. Satisfied, a happy smile curving her lips, she turned and made her way downstairs with quick, eager footsteps to join her waiting lover.

"Lee!" His eyes lighting up with pleasure and admiration, Jake came forward and took her arm, touching his lips to her cheek. "You look absolutely beautiful. Each time I set eyes on you, you astound me afresh with how wonderful you look."

"You always look pretty good yourself, Jake," she returned dizzily, trying to keep it light. "Whether you're dressed up like now in a formal suit, or wearing just jeans and T-shirt. . . ."

"Or nothing at all?" he queried, with an impudent grin that sent her pulse rate soaring.

"Don't be conceited," she told him severely.

"I was only asking."

"You were fishing for compliments, and I'm not rising to the bait."

She had expected to find Jake's white Mercedes parked outside in the forecourt, and was surprised when he said they were walking. She discovered the reason why, only a couple of hundred yards along the esplanade, when he led her up the steps of an imposing Victorian mansion.

"My flat is on the second floor," he told her as he opened the paneled front door. "I hope . . . I think you'll like it, Lee."

Two minutes later she was assuring him that she did. It was spacious, with lofty rooms and tall windows both at the front and back of the house, giving splendid views of sea and town and mountains. As a bachelor's apartment it lacked some of the softening touches a woman would add, but it was extremely comfortable, with a large settee and several armchairs upholstered in cream leather, and bright rugs scattered on the parquet floor. The walls were painted in a pale avocado-green, which beautifully set off the polished wood of some elegant pieces of furniture. Lee paused by a particularly fine secretaire-cabinet of, she guessed, cherrywood, which was inlaid with birds and classical designs in lighter wood, and topped with a scrolled and fretted pediment.

"What marvelous craftsmanship," she exclaimed, running her fingertips over the satiny surface.

"Thank you, ma'am."

Lee looked at him in surprise. "You mean this is your own work, Jake? I took it for an antique."

"Which it is," he said, "and hopefully I've managed to restore it to what it was when new. It's an American piece, made, I believe, around 1800 in Rhode Island. How it came to be over here I've no idea. Perhaps a ship's captain brought it back as a present for his wife. When I found it—rescued it—it had been used for many years as a cupboard in the kitchen of a farmhouse. It was virtually unrecognizable, in a terrible state. Someone had even daubed on a thick coat of some horrible dark varnish."

"What sacrilege!" Lee cried in horror. "You've done it

so beautifully, Jake. I can't even feel where the two different woods are joined. It's on a par with the fine work you did restoring *Lancashire Lass*. You must have a great love of wood."

"Working with it gives me a lot of pleasure and satisfaction. I guess I'm never happier . . . no, that's not true." He grinned meaningfully. "I can think of occasions when the pleasure of using my hands on mere wood pales into insignificance."

Lee colored pink, and moved to the door, saying, "Show me the rest of your flat. Y‑‑ really do have a lovely home here, Jake."

"You infinitely grace it with your presence, my lovely Lee."

The low, throbbing timbre of his voice made her turn from the door to face him. Slowly, as in a trancelike dream, their suddenly inflamed bodies drew nearer until, with a shuddering sigh from each of them, they were embracing, pressed close together, her breasts crushed against the rock wall of his chest. Jake ground his hips against hers and she felt his body tremble with arousal. Her mouth was claimed by his, lips and tongues melding in a fever of passion, and Lee's senses spun in a dizzying upward spiral of longing.

"Oh God, Lee," he groaned raggedly. "I want you so much. It's been an age since Saturday . . . a torment to live through."

"Yes, Jake, yes," she whispered. For her, too, it had been a tormenting age. Yes, yes, she needed him as intensely as he needed her.

Jake said with a shaky laugh, "I mustn't deprive you of your dinner."

"Dinner?" she murmured vaguely, food the very last thing on her mind.

"Come and see."

The dining alcove was an L-shaped leg of the big living room that she hadn't so far noticed. The table was set with two places, a large wooden bowl of salad, cheese and fruit.

"It will spoil if we don't eat it now," Jake explained.

"What will spoil? Something you bought at the delicatessen?"

"Do you mind! I'm a dab hand at cooking, as well you know. Or did subsequent events at my cottage that night drive the meal we'd just eaten right out of your mind?"

"I've forgotten nothing," she said, with a shiver of recollection.

"You're sure? For instance, do you remember this?" He slipped his hands 'round to the nape of her neck caressingly, then drew her honey-blond hair forward to frame her face in a silken cloud, bending his head to nuzzle into the fragrant softness. "And this?" His hands moved to her breasts, teasing the nipples through the thin fabric of her dress and bra until they stood out swollen and hard.

"Jake!" she moaned from deep in her throat.

"And even this?" One hand slid lower, tenderly traversing the soft plane of her stomach to settle over the throbbing core of her desire. "I reverence every inch of your beautiful body," he breathed huskily. "Every curve and every tiny dimple; the smooth, firm flesh, so vibrantly alive and warm and exciting. I glory in this spun-silk hair of yours, these wide eyes that glint and gleam like sapphires, your enticing mouth, your whole lovely womanly being. I am drunk on your beauty, Lee."

They stood for long, pulsating moments, locked together, hands exploring one another in a feverish, erotic journey. Then Jake raised his head and sniffed the air.

"I'm very much afraid that our dinner is burning. I won't be a moment."

As he disappeared through a door to the kitchen, an appetizing aroma wafted to Lee's nostrils. She took the chance to straighten herself, scoop her hair back into place and check her appearance in a mirror. Her face looked flushed; her eyes were burning brightly.

Jake returned bearing an oval platter on which rested an interesting-looking shape of puff pastry, just a shade browner than ideal. "I think I caught it in time," he said. "If not, Lee darling, you only have yourself to blame, for being altogether too delectable for a man to resist."

"What is it we're eating?" she asked. "It smells heavenly."

"*Le saumon en croûte,* if chosen from the menu of a fancy restaurant. At home, a very simple dish consisting of a nice large fillet of fresh Welsh salmon with a pinch of this and a twist of that, encased in pastry from the supermarket and popped into the oven. There, you've wheedled from me the secret of my culinary skill."

"The skill," she said with a laugh, "lies in the pinch of this and the twist of that. It looks and smells fantastic, Jake. You could have been a chef if you'd wanted a different career."

They sat side by side at the table, facing a window overlooking the yacht haven and beyond that the open sea. On the horizon, where the sun had recently set, the sky was a fiery glory of crimson and gold. With a flourish, Jake neatly dissected the pastry case, and served them each a large portion.

"Hey!" Lee protested. "That's far too much for me."

"Rubbish! It's important for you to . . . to fuel your energy. Help yourself to salad."

From a side table Jake lifted across an ice bucket in which nestled a bottle of champagne. He popped the cork and filled two glasses.

"You're really doing things in style," she remarked.

"What else, for such a stylish lady?" He handed her a glass, and raised his own to her in a toast. "Here's to you, Lee darling. Did I ever tell you that you're beautiful?"

"And did I ever tell you that you're a handsome devil?"

They smiled into one another's eyes. And when their lips met in a kiss that lingered and deepened, it felt to Lee as if the champagne bubbles were fizzing through her veins.

Presently, almost reluctantly, they began to eat. Lee was surprised to find that her appetite, jaded for the past two days, was keen and zestful for the excellent food. The feather-light pastry made a deliciously crisp counterpoint to the succulent pink flakes of salmon. The salad dressing was sharply astringent, the champagne cool and refreshing and exhilarating.

Outside the window, the western sky was now a smoky, fading pink. But the moon was coming up, etching the roofs of the town with silver light, casting ink-black shadows. They sat on, with just the faint orange glow of a single table lamp across the room. Jake's hand held hers loosely, playing in turn with each slender finger. She thrilled to the faint rasp of his rougher male skin.

"Have you had enough?" he asked softly.

"Oh yes, plenty."

"Well, I haven't," Jake said with a significant laugh. He rose to his feet, drawing her up with him, and they moved toward the center of the room. Momentarily, he turned away to press a switch, and the air throbbed with a soft, romantic melody. They began to dance, swaying together, hips thrust to hips, their bodies pulsing with the beat of the music.

"Happy?" Jake asked her.

"Yes, oh yes!" It was true, as of now. She had shut out the future. There was only the present moment, she dancing in his arms. And tonight, being together.

"I want you to be happy, Lee." His voice was husky, pitched low, with a vibrant timbre. "I long to make you happy."

"You do," she whispered. "You will, Jake."

Their slow dancing carried them purposefully, thrillingly, out of the door and into his bedroom, with the throbbing tempo of the music pursuing them faintly. Here, they stood together at the window, watching the veils of gossamer cloud riding across the face of the moon that had risen to hang above the mountains, bathing them in its quicksilver light. Then, with one accord, they turned and clung to each other in a sudden fever of rising desire. Jake's fingers were at the zipper of her dress, hers at the lapels of his jacket, pushing it from his shoulders. He paused briefly to shake it free and fling it aside, then the dress was being peeled away from her and eased over her hips until that too was on the floor and she was left in just bra and panties. But even then there still seemed far too much clothing as a barrier between them. With eager fingers she slid off his necktie, then felt impatiently for the buttons of his shirt, finally tugging it out from the restricting waistband of his trousers. Thankfully, she pressed her palms to the hot skin of his contoured chest, and laid her cheek against his throat.

"Oh, my darling . . ." he whispered brokenly, his arms tightening around her, his lips finding hers.

Moments later, Jake turned her with a swift, insistent movement, and she felt the clasp of her bra unfasten. Gently he disposed of the wispy garment and, sighing with pleasure, cupped her liberated breasts in the hollow of his hands, while his lips nuzzled against the soft curve of her neck.

"My darling," he murmured again. "Your body is so sweet and perfect. I can think of nothing but you, of making love to you, of possessing you."

Her reply was lost in the tautness of her throat as she

broke away from his adoring grasp to face him again, fumbling with too much haste for the buckle of his leather belt, the zipper, dragging trousers and underbriefs across the firm mold of his buttocks and down the long, hard shafts of his thighs. His shoes and socks were a momentary hitch which was quickly dealt with, then he was magnificently naked. As she rose to her feet again, a slant of moonlight fell across his body, and she thrilled at the sight of his muscled perfection. At some almost unnoticed moment her panties had gone, too, and they stood pressed against each other, skin to skin, their hands roaming in a restless giving and receiving of erotic pleasure, their mouths joined in a drowning, never-ending kiss. The music had long since come to a stop, but they had no need of it; they wouldn't have heard it anyway above the loud drumming of their heartbeats and the wild crescendo of their coda of passion.

Eons of lost time later they found themselves upon the bed. The moon, in its silent passage across the sky, spilled its pale silver light where their two bodies lay with arms and legs entwined, Jake's hard, yearning body pulsing its message through to her, bringing a spiraling urgency to her own need.

"Jake, I love you!" No, she hadn't actually spoken the words beyond a silent whisper in her head. She let herself bask in the warm emotion of her love, pushing to the farthermost edge of her mind the knowledge that Jake didn't love her in return. He wanted her—wanted her desperately—*that* she believed. But he didn't love her. The only kind of genuine love he felt was for the skill of his artistic hands manipulating wood.

Even this slight distraction from her perfect happiness was banished when Jake laid a hand across the flat curve of her stomach, and bent to touch the pointed tip of his tongue to the shell-like hollow of her navel. With fluttering fingertips he drew sensuous patterns on her flesh. His hands caressed her steadily with sweet remorselessness. Lee responded with wild, sobbing cries of rapture at his endless coaxing that continued in a steady rhythm as the tide of passion in her rose higher and ever higher toward the promise of ecstasy.

"Jake," she gasped breathlessly. "Oh Jake . . . it's so wonderful."

His lips trailed a scorching path of tiny kisses down the curving line of her chin and throat, onward down until he captured her breast with his mouth, softly enclosing her warm flesh and caressing the hardened peak with little flicks of his tongue to bring her fresh waves of shivering delight. Then his mouth moved on again, all over her body. Almost delirious by now, Lee arched herself against the electrifying probe of his tongue, while his hands stroked the firm, yielding roundness of her buttocks.

Then . . . she cried out his name over and over into the silent, moonlit darkness of the room, while her body writhed and twisted in a paroxysm of shuddering joy . . . joy without end, it seemed, as she lost grip on reality and her only awareness was of this erotic heaven with Jake. On and on until, with a gasp of incredulous delight, she felt her glowing body suddenly blaze alight and she was sent spiraling into space.

Long drifting-down moments later, when she lay still and quiet, Jake raised his head and smiled at her. He enfolded her in his arms. His lips touched her mouth in a mark of tenderness, pride and pleasure, and he kissed away the wetness on her cheeks.

"My wonderful darling!" he breathed huskily. "Even your tears taste sweet. I'm glad that I made you happy."

"You did, oh how you did! You give me such exquisite pleasure, you can't imagine."

His own desire had not yet been assuaged. Lee reached up her mouth to find his lips and kissed him boldly, provocatively, while her fingers ran a feathered course down the heated flesh of his body. When she touched him as she knew he yearned to be touched, Jake shuddered in a moan of ecstasy.

"I want you, Lee. I want you now, my darling."

"Yes, now . . . now," she said on a snatched breath. She drew him to her tenderly, offering herself in total submissive surrender. With a sure, swift movement Jake fused their bodies together. His breathing was fast and ragged, his movements becoming quicker and less controlled. Lee sensed he was doing battle with the frenzied pitch of his longing, but he was goaded on by raw desire and there could be no holding back. He cried out her name and it was a ringing shout of male abandon combined with a plea for her understanding and forgiveness. In the grip of unleashed passion he thrust and thrust into her until, with a violent spasm that shook through the length of his body, he cried out once more and became still. She felt his warm skin under her fingers, and it was damp with sweat. The male scent of him was sweet in her nostrils.

In the moonlight, Jake's dark eyes glittered as he raised himself to look down at her.

"I'm sorry, Lee darling."

"What are you sorry for, you silly?" Lovingly, she traced the strong line of his jaw with one finger. "You were wonderful."

"I lost control," he said humbly.

"I wanted you to. I wanted, that time, to be taken, possessed, used entirely for your pleasure."

"I'll make it up to you, I promise." His breath was still coming fast, and his heartbeat thudded. "You're a lovely, strange girl, Lee."

"Strange?"

"Most women," he explained, "don't consider the way the man feels. They merely use him as a means to their own fulfillment. He is forced to take, because nothing is freely given. Whereas with you . . ."

He was terribly wrong. Any woman in love would always put her man first, above herself. But Lee remained silent, afraid that by voicing this truth she would betray herself.

"You were wonderful, Jake," she whispered again. "Each time with you, I've glimpsed a heaven I never knew existed."

"You're quite unlike any other woman I've ever met, Lee darling. Making love with you is on a different plane, in another sphere. I've never before known such intensity of feeling."

Lee snuggled up against him, her hand resting lightly on the firm column of his thigh. Despite this glorious afterglow of happiness, a wistful strand of another, sadder emotion wove insidiously into her thoughts. This night had to mark the end of her briefly blossoming relationship with Jake. There could be no question of spending any more glorious nights like this with him. She had allowed herself this one last time in order to carry away an even stronger memory of him, but to see him again tomorrow or on Thursday evening would constitute a pandering to weakness she could not permit herself. Soon . . . before they parted, she would tell Jake and make him understand.

How quickly, she wondered bleakly, would he replace her with another woman? She believed what he'd just said about making love with her . . . that it was a new level of experience for him. But now he would take this as his new standard, to be equalled or exceeded. There would be plenty of choice available to him. The number of women ready and eagerly willing to accept a devastatingly attractive man like Jake Talbot as a bed partner had to be limitless.

Lee gave herself a tiny shake. She had gone into this

continuing affair with Jake with her eyes wide open. He had not hidden from her the kind of man he was; he had made her no promises. She had always known it must end sooner or later, so it would be weak and foolish to shed tears now that the end was approaching. . . .

She roused herself from a dreamy doze to find the bedroom bathed in the soft light of a shaded lamp. Jake was gone from the bed and she was alone. Hearing a slight sound, she turned and saw him gazing down at her. He wore a short dark-blue dressing robe, the sash carelessly tied around his waist.

"Hi, sleepyhead," he said.

"Hi yourself!" She was still muddleheaded from sleep, and the languor of their recent loving was still heavy in her limbs.

He sat on the edge of the bed, bending to kiss her lips. From the pocket of his robe he took a flat, dark-green velvet box and held it out to her.

"My sweet Lee, I want you to have this."

"What is it?"

"Open it, and see."

She sat up and did as he said. When she touched the tiny clasp and raised the hinged lid, she found, nestling in ruched black satin, a gold chain with a large pendant that was richly encrusted with glittering diamonds.

"But I don't understand. . . ." she said, frowning.

Taking it out of the box, Jake slipped the chain around her neck so that the gold pendant hung between her naked breasts, its diamonds glinting in the lamplight.

"It looks beautiful on you," he murmured, and bent to press a soft kiss to her creamy throat. "It will be something to remind you of me, always."

"Are you . . . are you trying to give this to me?" Lee faltered in dismay.

"What else, darling?"

"I . . . I can't possibly accept it, Jake."

Putting his lips to the tumbled silk of her hair, he murmured, "Give me one good reason why you can't."

"But it's obviously very valuable. . . ."

"And you imagine that you don't deserve it?"

Lee felt so shocked, so horrified, that for a moment she was at a loss what to say to him. Then her anger came surging to the surface. "Deserve it for what?" she spat out harshly. "For services rendered?"

"Lee," he protested, "you're being foolish." He moved to take her into his arms, but she fended him off. Quickly, she dragged the pendant over her head and dropped it into his lap. Then, suddenly aware of her nakedness, she drew up the sheet to cover herself.

"*Being* foolish?" she echoed on a hysterical note. "I've *been* foolish . . . terribly foolish. But not anymore. Now, kindly leave me so that I can get dressed."

"But Lee . . ."

"Didn't you hear me?" she snapped. "I asked you to get out."

Jake seemed about to argue further, then he shrugged and rose to his feet. "Okay, I'll go and make us some coffee." Pausing to scoop up his own clothes, which still lay where they'd been dropped to the floor, he walked out of the room and closed the door behind him.

In her misery Lee flopped back against the pillows and lay there struggling to keep the tears from falling. Jake's action in offering her a fabulously expensive payoff gift had in a single stroke robbed their brief romance of all its beauty. It now became a bitter, sordid episode, to be erased as soon as possible from her memory. Except that she would never be able to forget.

She steeled herself. If she lay lingering here, Jake would come back before she was dressed and she didn't want that to happen. With a shuddering sigh, she threw back the bedcovers and put her feet to the floor. It was hateful having to re-don the silk jersey dress which she'd chosen deliberately to be seductive, to entice Jake, but she had no option. She spent minutes at the mirror on his tallboy, doing what she could with her fingers to straighten her hair and remove the tousled look that was a legacy of their passion.

It took courage to leave the bedroom and join Jake. With her hand on the knob she stood hesitating for several moments before decisively opening the door and going through to the living room.

"I'm leaving now, Jake," she told him, standing at the threshold.

He swung 'round from where he'd been setting a coffee tray on a low table. "But you can't leave like this. I won't let you."

"I'll decide for myself when I leave," she said with a flare of anger, "and it's going to be now."

Jake came striding across the room, reaching for her. But Lee held up a forbidding hand. "No, don't touch me!" She put steely resolve into her voice. "I was going to tell you, in any case, that tonight would be . . . the last time. We could have parted friends, with good memories. But now . . . you've made me feel cheap, tainted."

"For God's sake," he protested. "Are you out of your senses, Lee?"

"No, I've just come to my senses. I'm not about to cry over what can't be changed, Jake, but from this moment on I want nothing more to do with you except for what is strictly business."

He ran a hand through his still-tousled dark hair in bewilderment. "I don't believe this. All because I wanted to give you a bit of jewelry."

"A bit of jewelry worth hundreds of pounds at the very least."

"What's that got to do with anything?" he demanded.

"My God! The fact that you can even ask such a

question proves that you're totally insensitive. If you'd bought me some small thing . . . a pretty brooch or bracelet, something simple and inexpensive, I could have accepted it as a token of your—" She almost said "a token of your love." Just in time, she amended it to, "your affection for me. But that pendant is something else altogether, in a totally different category. By offering it to me you've insured one thing . . . that I'll never forget Jake Talbot as long as I live. The memory of you will serve as an ominous warning."

His angular, sculpted face was dark and drawn. "You're getting all this wildly out of proportion, Lee."

"Am I? What was your scenario, Jake? That I'd joyfully accept the valuable pendant, not realizing that it was a payoff? That soon, in your own good time, you'd break the news to me that it was all over between us. And I would weep and plead, leaving you with a great feeling of what a terrific, sexy guy you are, able to get a silly female totally hooked on you. Have I got it right?"

His expression was like stone as he grated, "No, you've got it all wrong."

"Really?" She threw him a look of open scorn. "You can't pretend that you haven't given thought to the way our relationship would eventually end. And when."

Jake was silent, a strange, bewildered look in his eyes that was part anger and part pain. Lee felt reckless, heady with the knowledge that she in turn could inflict wounds.

"Perhaps you imagined," she said in a scathing tone, "that after I leave here at the end of this week, it could continue on a nice, comfortable, casual basis . . . very convenient for you. I'd be here in Aberdyffryn every now and then as work on the factory extensions progressed, and in between times you would keep yourself amused with various other girlfriends."

"Damn you, Lee!" he rasped.

"This may astound you," she continued implacably, "but the purpose of my existence on this earth doesn't happen to be to feed your male vanity. I was stupid enough to believe that we'd achieved something worthwhile, Jake, however shortlived it was fated to be."

"And wasn't it worthwhile?" he ground out.

"Oh, I won't deny for a moment that you're a magnificent bedmate. For a woman seeking sensual thrills, and who can shut her eyes to the real truth, I doubt if there's anyone to surpass you."

His jaw tightened and it was as if a shutter came down over his dark eyes. After a momentary pause, he asked in a toneless voice, "And what is this real truth about me that you think you've discovered, Lee?"

"Making love is just a game to you, Jake . . . a game at which you must excel. When you hold a woman in your arms, when you delight her with your skillful hands, is it *her* pleasure you're really concerned with, or just getting a smug feeling of satisfaction at your own brilliant performance?"

"That's a vile thing to say," he exploded.

"I rather think," she said quietly, all at once strangely in command of herself, "that what you do is even more vile. There's no way I can prevent you from making other women unhappy, Jake—you will, that's inevitable—but not me any more. Good-bye!"

As she went to collect her patent-leather evening bag from the settee, Jake moved across to the door and stood blocking her exit. For long, unnerving moments they glared at one another, then, with an indifferent shrug, he stood aside.

"Very well then, go!" he growled out savagely.

Lee hesitated, her heart fluttering. Even now, she found it hard to believe that the end could be like this, so ugly, so brutal, after the two of them had shared such joy.

She felt the ache of unshed tears as, with fragile care, she crossed the lobby and let herself out of Jake's flat.

On the esplanade, the evening wind had freshened. The moon was hidden now by a bank of clouds. With purposeful footsteps, she walked back briskly to her hotel.

9

Lee lay in her bed during that long, restless night, conscious of the endless wash of waves on the beach below. Previously, it had seemed to her a friendly, reassuring sound. Now it was cold and bleak, without hope. Her tortured dreams had been haunted by the phantom figures of herself and Jake reenacting that final, horrible scene, over and over.

She roused at seven-thirty to the pot of morning tea that she normally enjoyed, brought to her room by a chatty young chambermaid.

"A nasty, drizzly morning it is," the girl announced cheerfully, flicking back the curtains.

"That's good," Lee replied unthinkingly.

"Good? Well, surprised I am that anyone should like the rain. But there it is, it takes all sorts."

"Oh, I didn't mean . . ." Lee shrugged. It wasn't worth trying to sort out the confusion. "Thank you for the tea, Dorcas."

"Welcome you are, Mrs. Jordan."

Getting dressed, having breakfast, Lee searched for the strength to brave the day ahead. How was she going to face up to an encounter with Jake? To avoid him would mean keeping clear of the factory, and she refused such a cowardly way out. Architect and client they would be, and nothing more. If that didn't suit Jake, then he could always dispense with the services of Hammond and Jordan.

Arriving at Talbot Woodcraft, she tried to apply her mind to one of the problems she still hadn't resolved—the most economical site for the service elevators to assist a smooth production flow. But as the morning drifted on it seemed as if her brain was numb, frozen, shell-shocked; she couldn't make her thoughts follow any coherent line. She began to despair, feeling that the job here was altogether beyond her now.

Around eleven o'clock she was called to the phone with the message that Mr. Hammond wanted to speak to her. The thought of talking to Ashley right now was too daunting, and she asked that he be told she was unavailable. But when he persisted by calling again a half-hour later while she was in the upholstery workshop, she reluctantly gave in.

"Everything going smoothly, darling?" he inquired when they'd exchanged greetings, adding the endearment with quiet deliberation.

Lee sighed heavily. Suddenly Ashley, too, had become a big problem. It was going to be tricky to make him understand that she wasn't the woman for him without its affecting the future harmony of their professional partnership.

"You sound down in the dumps," he went on, when she didn't immediately answer his question. "You've been working too darned hard, that's what it is."

Lee felt a stab of conscience. There were no two ways

about it—this job at Talbot Woodcraft had gone all to hell. The realization suddenly crashed down on her that she hadn't a hope of pulling together a decent presentation of her ideas in time for the meeting with Jake scheduled for Friday.

"Ashley, I . . . I'm not sure that I can meet the deadline."

"That's very unlike you!" He sounded surprised rather than put out. "What's the trouble, Lee? Have you encountered unexpected problems?"

"Well . . . yes."

"What, for instance?"

"Oh, nothing I can especially pinpoint. It's just . . . well, this is one of those assignments that won't seem to go right."

"I know how it is," said Ashley sympathetically. "Listen, darling, I'll still come on Friday, as arranged, and we'll put our heads together. You're the expert on this sort of project, of course, but a new viewpoint might just possibly find the answer to some of the snags you've struck. Meantime, you have a word with Jake Talbot and reschedule our meeting with him for one day next week."

"Oh no!" The complications of her life suddenly seemed to have redoubled, overwhelming her. The prospect of having to contend with Ashley's presence over the weekend was bad enough. But much, much worse, she just couldn't face spending several more days in such close proximity to Jake. Desperately, she tried to get herself together and become brisk. "Listen Ashley, there's no need for any drastic changes in our plans. I . . . I expect I was exaggerating a bit. After all, I still have forty-eight hours left, and I'll just have to pull out all the stops."

Ashley argued with her in an amiable way for a few minutes longer. But she detected a note of relief in his voice when she finally insisted that he really needn't worry, she'd cope somehow or other. Ashley himself was a very efficient person, always well organized if a trifle overfussy about detail, and it would worry him no end to think that his partner had allowed things to slide out of control.

"By the way," he went on, "have you seen much of Talbot?"

That threw Lee badly. "Er . . . why do you ask?"

"Well, you know what I always say about socializing with clients. There's never any harm in oiling the wheels a bit. I thought perhaps he would have taken you out to lunch or something."

"As a matter of fact he did," she said, treading warily. "We . . . we also had dinner together last night."

"That's fine!" Then Ashley gave a soft chuckle, and said, "But don't go overdoing the palsiness with him, darling, or I'll get jealous."

She gave a weak laugh of dismissal, hoping it conveyed the right neutral attitude. As she said good-bye to Ashley and hung up the wall phone, she found that her palms were damp and she was trembling. Then, to add the final straw, no sooner was she back to taking measurements than the swing doors at the far end of the long upholstery workshop were flung open to admit Jake. Panicking at the sight of him, Lee turned and fled through the other exit and out of the building.

With no real sense of purpose, she found herself walking quickly along the street that led to the seafront. She glanced at her wristwatch. 11:45. The best thing would be to take an early lunch break—not that she had any appetite—and make a fresh start this afternoon. There was a slight misting of rain in the air, but Lee ignored it, vaguely thinking that she'd dive into the first suitable place and buy a sandwich.

For a while she hardly noticed that the rain had been getting heavier. Soon, though, it was coming down in earnest and soaking through her thin cotton dress to the skin. By good fortune, the Prince of Wales Hotel was only a short distance away. Lee broke into a run, hurrying up the hotel steps and pushing in through the revolving doors. She collected her room key from the desk and was heading for the staircase when a drawling voice from behind arrested her.

"You look somewhat bedraggled and forlorn, Lee, to say the least."

Lee spun 'round to meet the mocking gaze of Merle Channon. The other woman, looking tall, elegant and poised, was standing in the doorway of her boutique, which opened directly off the foyer.

"The rain took me by surprise," Lee explained, with a careless shrug.

Merle's eyes were questioning. "I didn't realize that you came back to the hotel at midday. Are you intending to have lunch here?"

"Oh no, I rarely have more than a sandwich during the day. I find a big meal in the evening quite enough." Her intention was to put the damper on any idea Merle might have of their eating together. She could do without a rerun of the other night.

Far from seeming disappointed by this response, though, Merle looked rather pleased. Letting her gaze scan Lee's figure, she remarked, "No doubt you're wise to cut down on the calories. I don't need to bother, of course. I never put on an ounce of surplus flesh, however much I eat."

"Lucky you!"

"Aren't I just!"

To any observer, it might have been a friendly exchange. Only Lee could read the malice in those smiling green-gold eyes. Only she herself knew the bitter hatred she felt in her heart for Merle.

"I'd advise you," Merle continued, "to get out of those wet things before you catch a chill."

Lee gritted her teeth. "That was precisely what I was trying to do when you stopped me."

"Oh dear, have I been holding you up? Believe me, Lee, that's the last thing I'd want to do. See you around another day, I daresay. *Ciao!*" With that, she turned and vanished into the boutique.

Lee, her fists clenched tight with frustrated fury, made her way up to her room. She found herself shivering, and it was only partly from the dampness of her clothes. Undressing, she took a stinging hot shower, then put on a skirt and sweater which would be more appropriate for today's weather than another dress. Her raincoat was in the car, so she slipped on her navy blazer and took a small folding umbrella for further protection.

Scorning the temptation to linger here in the safe cocoon of her room, Lee resolutely made her way downstairs. She had forgotten any thought of food by now; she was intent on returning as quickly as possible to Talbot Woodcraft and putting in a long afternoon. If she chanced to see Jake around the factory, she wouldn't be such a fool as to panic again, but would acknowledge him formally and then ignore him.

It was a relief to find no sign of Merle in the lobby. Lee dropped her room key at the desk and turned to head for the revolving doors to the street. At that instant she heard a woman's laugh, a ringing, penetrating sound. Merle, without question. Lee glanced around before she could check herself and, through the velvet-draped archway to the cocktail bar, she glimpsed those derisive green-gold eyes of Merle's glinting a message of triumph. Sitting with her at a small table was Jake. Merle had her hand possessively on his shoulder, and they'd obviously been sharing a joke. In that frozen moment of time, Lee stood rigidly still, staring, while Jake half turned his head and looked directly at her. His face was set in a rock-hard expression, conveying not the smallest interest in her, beyond contempt.

This encounter had been deliberately planned by Merle, of course. Easy enough to check that Lee was still in the hotel from the absence of her key from its hook behind the desk. Easy enough to choose a table just inside the cocktail lounge from which Merle could see and be seen. That penetrating laugh had been timed to the split-second to catch Lee's attention.

Somehow Lee found the strength to make her legs function and she walked on, crossing the lobby and pushing her way through the revolving doors. Outside, the rain had ceased. She crossed the esplanade and stood clutching the ornamental railings above the beach, staring out at the swirling sea, steely-gray now under massed storm clouds. How good it would be, she thought wretchedly, to float away on that great emptiness and find peace, find blessed oblivion.

Taking a grip on herself, Lee directed her footsteps back to Talbot Woodcraft. She had work to do, a job to finish. But as the afternoon wore on she achieved less than nothing, and she came to the humiliating realization that she just couldn't go on. Arguments turned and twisted in her mind, slowly edging her toward a decision to quit. It would be the first time in her life that she'd ever walked out on an assignment, but it was one time that there seemed no alternative. How could she face those scornful eyes of Jake's across his office desk, with Ashley sitting there alongside her, and present him with a report on her suggestions about the extensions? She felt ill at the thought of it.

But if she did throw in her hand, what would she tell Ashley? The truth about her tawdry affair with Jake was out of the question. Then she reflected, with a flash of irritation, why should I need to justify my every decision to my business partner? I'm entitled to the occasional impulsive action, for heaven's sake. It wasn't as if the firm of Hammond and Jordan were desperate for commissions. They had plenty of other work lined up. True, this particular job would be quite prestigious; a sensitively executed addition to an old building always was. Of course, if Hammond and Jordan did abandon the project at this stage, Jake could always make waves, claiming against them for a damaging loss of time. But she doubted if he'd do that. Jake would, she thought with a shiver of misery, be only too thankful to see the back of her.

Oddly, the heartbreaking factor that finally tipped the scales was not the image of Jake, with his face harsh set and his eyes contemptuously glacial. It was the suddenly returning memory of Merle, seated beside him in the cocktail bar, her hand possessively on his shoulder. Hastily scooping up her various papers and stuffing them into her briefcase, Lee looked in the works manager's office to tell a surprised Dylan Lambert that she was returning at once to Bristol and would be getting in touch.

What did it matter, Lee thought desolately as she got in her car and headed toward the hotel again, that she was handing Merle the victory on a silver platter? Merle had already won, anyway. And this way it wouldn't be necessary ever to set eyes on Jake again. An exchange of letters, coolly polite from her, no doubt angry and hostile from him. Then it would all be over. She didn't permit her thoughts to look farther into a future that would be bleak and gray and pointless.

Lee packed her bags carelessly, taking little trouble to fold her clothes. The jacket and jeans and matelot sweater she'd bought in Merle's boutique she stuffed into the trash bin, hardly able to bring herself even to handle them. She rang for a porter and told him to put her luggage in her car. After a last glance around to check that she'd forgotten nothing in her haste, she went downstairs and called for her bill.

"You were planning to stay with us until the end of the week, Mrs. Jordan," the clerk observed. "There's nothing wrong, I hope, to cause you to depart early?"

"No, nothing wrong," she said with a bright, false smile. "Just a change of plans."

The rain started again with relentless persistence as Lee left Aberdyffryn behind her and headed into the mountains. Already the light was failing, the sky above the rugged peaks a menacing gun-metal gray. It had become close, humid, and Lee was not surprised to see flashes of lightning and hear thunder echo through the valleys.

There was little other traffic. Occasionally, headlights blazed out of the gloom ahead and a car or truck flashed by, sending a slap of spray across her windshield. Lee passed through a small, huddled village, and looked with longing at the warmth of lighted windows.

The storm worsened. The rain was coming down in sheets and the road was awash with water. She was forced to slow, the beams of her headlamps stabbing only a feeble pathway through the murk. In the rear-view mirror she became aware of the lights of a car behind her. It was gaining fast, she realized, and she wondered what kind of maniac would drive at such speed in this weather.

The other car was upon her, overtaking her with a roar and a dazzle of light. Dimly, she was aware that it was white; the figure at the wheel just a vague blur. Drawing ahead, the car braked and stopped. A figure jumped out and stood in the middle of the road flagging her down. It was Jake.

Stunned, Lee watched as he ran up to her car and dragged the door open, letting water spatter in on her.

"What the hell d'you think you're up to?" he demanded.

"What does it look like?" she retorted, though her heart was thudding a wild drumbeat within her ribcage. "I'm hardly out for a joyride in this weather."

Already Jake's dark hair was sodden, and water streamed down his leanly carved face. But he seemed oblivious to this.

"Are you running out on me?" he asked incredulously.

"I'm quitting the job at Talbot Woodcraft," she corrected. "There was no sense carrying on with it, Jake. I've no interest in it anymore, so I couldn't hope to do a decent job for you. And you certainly can't want to have me hanging around any longer."

"I don't give a curse about you quitting the job," he snarled.

"Good. Then I don't need to feel guilty about it."

"It's you that I care about, Lee. You and me."

She stared up at him in total amazement. "You surely can't still have ideas in that direction? Not after last night."

"Last night went horribly wrong," he growled.

"Yes Jake, it did," she agreed, fighting her pain at the bittersweet memories. "You slipped up by revealing just how you viewed our relationship, and made me feel horribly cheap and bought."

Impatiently, he put a hand on her shoulder, and gave her a push. "Move over!"

"You're not getting in this car," she protested.

"Yes, I am. So move over." This time his push had more weight behind it, and Lee yielded, sliding awkwardly across into the passenger seat. Jake folded his long length into the small car and pulled the door shut.

"That's better. Now we can talk . . . get things sorted out."

"There's nothing to sort out."

"On the contrary, there's a hell of a lot." He ran his hands across his face to clear away the raindrops. "Lee, I was a fool to give you the pendant the way I did."

"You miscalculated more than somewhat," she said scornfully. "That sort of thing might work with some women, but not with me."

"I've never done anything remotely like it before."

"No?"

"No!" he said explosively.

"Then why pick on me for the doubtful honor of being the first woman you've tried to pay off with an expensive gift?"

Jake put his hands behind his head, rubbing his neck as if it ached. "You've got it all confused, Lee. That pendant belonged to my mother. It was the only valuable piece of jewelry she ever owned. My father bought it for her one Christmas as an extra-special gift, after he'd achieved a mild prosperity with Talbot Woodcraft. I've treasured it always because I can picture her, looking so dazzlingly beautiful in my young boy's eyes, when she got dressed up for a special occasion."

Lee felt bewildered. "Then why on earth, if the pendant is so precious to you, did you try to give it away to me?"

In the glimmer of light from the dashboard she could discern the expression on Jake's sculpted face, but it was one that she couldn't interpet. "If you'd asked me that question last night, Lee, I couldn't have answered. I gave you that pendant on an impulse, a pure whim. When I came to after we'd made love and saw you lying asleep beside me looking so beautiful, with a smile on your lips and your marvelous hair spread out over the pillow, I felt very moved. I wanted to do something . . . try to make you understand how I felt about you—even though I didn't properly understand myself. My mother's pendant suddenly flashed into my mind, and an overwhelming urge made me go and fetch it to give you."

"That doesn't make sense," she said dazedly. "You surely didn't imagine that I'd accept it?"

"I don't know what I thought," he confessed. "Looking back, I can see that you had to refuse to accept it. That—being you—you couldn't really have done otherwise. But I didn't stop to reason things out. I was incapable of rational thought at that time. It just suddenly came to me, very forcibly, that I wanted you to have my mother's pendant."

Lee swallowed hard and said faintly, "You talk as if you understand your motives better now, Jake."

"I do!" He turned in the seat, facing her, and she felt the warmth of his breath feathering her cheek. It made her feel weak with love for him, tense with the familiar aching tug of desire. "Like most seemingly complex questions," he added, "it has an exceedingly simple answer."

"Which is?" she dared to ask breathlessly.

"I love you, Lee darling. But I only realized it when I thought I'd lost you."

"Please don't say things you don't mean," she whispered, her tremulous voice almost drowned out by the thrumming of rain on the car roof. "It . . . it isn't fair."

"But it's true, I do love you. You've got to believe it, Lee." He leaned forward and buried his face into the soft curve of her neck. His hair was still sodden, but Lee scarcely even noticed that as she reached up to fondle it with her hands. "I was so shocked, Lee darling, when Dylan Lambert told me that you'd left the factory in a hurry this afternoon and were returning to Bristol. And then when I rang the hotel, I heard that you'd checked out, and I began to feel quite desperate. I called myself every kind of fool, and I came tearing after you just as fast as I possibly could. Thank God I caught up with you."

Despite her caressing fingers, her words had a stinging sharpness. "Jake, no tricks, for pity's sake. I just can't take any more. I had to quit the job because I couldn't bear the thought of staying in Aberdyffryn and being near you, even for just a few more days. Okay, so I might as well admit the truth to you now . . . the truth that I dared not let you guess at before, knowing that once you realized it I would be completely within your power. You say that you love me, Jake . . . that the knowledge came to you all of a sudden after you thought you'd lost me . . . only then, only when I'd escaped from your mesmerizing influence. But, Jake, I've loved you ever since we . . . ever since that night at your cottage. Afterwards, I knew that it could never have happened the way it did if I hadn't fallen in love with you instantly, at first sight."

"You love me, Lee?" He raised his face to seek her eyes in the faint, luminous glow of light. "But that's wonderful. Incredible! After what I did, my idiotic clumsiness, I was so scared that I'd made you hate me."

"You did," she said huskily. "I do hate you, in a way, Jake. Love and hate can exist side by side. You've taught me that."

"But that's crazy," he exclaimed, his hands gripping her shoulders. "Love is love. How can you possibly hate someone when you love him?"

"Very easily . . . when the person you love doesn't return your feelings. When he is incapable of truly loving anyone."

"But that's not true!" he protested vehemently.

"It is true, Jake," she said with a despairing sigh. "To you, I'm just another woman you've slept with, and whom you'd like to go on sleeping with for a while longer. I have to feel flattered, I suppose, that I rate as rather special with you. . . ."

"Much, much more than rather special—you're fantastic! Quite unique. You're everything I could possibly want in a woman. Let me show you, Lee darling . . . just let me prove how much you mean to me."

"In what way?" she asked in a scathing voice. "By more and still more sex? Can't you understand how trivial that is, Jake?"

"Trivial?" he echoed reproachfully. "For God's sake, Lee darling, it's you and me we're talking about. Were those times we spent together trivial . . . at the cottage, on the boat, last night in my apartment? There was something magical in the way our two bodies responded to each other. Can you deny it?"

She felt tears sting her eyes. "The way you're talking, Jake, just illustrates what I mean. You speak of love, when what you really mean is sex . . . good sex."

"They're one and the same thing," he contended.

"No," she insisted. "Sex is just *part* of being in love, not the whole of it. Love is made up of so many things it's impossible to list them off the cuff. Love is sharing, and wanting to share. Giving, but taking, too. Love is knowing that without the person you love, life would become a bleak, dragging existence. It's wanting to be together always, through bad times as well as good. It's being happy together, having fun together and dying a little each time you part. And sex, yes . . . wonderful, deeply fulfilling sex with just that one person and no one else."

"You doubt that I love you, darling," Jake said softly, "when all these things are what I feel for you?"

"You don't, Jake. How could you, when all the time

you keep up with another woman? And who knows how many others."

He sighed heavily. "Merle Channon again, I suppose? She never seems to stay out of our conversations for long."

"What do you expect? It's not just that you've gone on seeing her, but that you've discussed me with her. Laughed about me, even, from the sound of it."

"What on earth are you talking about now?" Jake asked, seeming genuinely bewildered.

"Merle knew all about us spending Saturday on the boat," she explained, unable to erase the bitterness from her voice. "She told me how proud you were of *Lancashire Lass* and how you couldn't resist showing it off to people."

"Whatever Merle knows about us spending Saturday together on the boat, it wasn't from me," Jake stated. "I've not discussed you with her at all, except to say that you're an architect here to plan the factory extension. And that I'm very impressed with your approach to the job."

His voice rang with sincerity, and Lee longed to believe that he was speaking the truth. Merle, she recalled, had used just that phrase about his being impressed with her as an architect—though Merle had made it sound as if Jake had a chauvinistic contempt for career women.

"How would she know about Saturday if you didn't tell her, Jake?"

He shrugged. "Aberdyffryn's a small place. Merle could have picked up that tidbit of information from any number of people."

"What does she want of you?" Lee asked dispiritedly. "Marriage?"

Jake gave a dry, humorless laugh. "If so, Merle can

think again. She's just about the last woman in the world I'd want to marry."

"But you've been having an affair with her, haven't you?"

"I don't deny it. Listen, Lee, I'm a fairly normal sort of male of my age and I've knocked around these past few years. I had no ties, no commitments, and when someone as sexily attractive as Merle Channon crossed my path and put herself on offer, it wasn't the sort of chance I passed up. She and I had a brief fling a while back, which couldn't be rated as particularly momentous for either of us, and since then we've got together a few odd times when we were both at loose ends."

"Besides which," Lee said scathingly, "it was to your advantage to keep up with Merle, right?"

"That had nothing whatever to do with it," Jake insisted. "Her father and I do business together because it makes sense for us both. He gets top quality furniture for his hotels at a cut-rate price, and I get a steady flow of work for the factory. I explained to you, didn't I, that times have been tough recently with foreign competition, and I've gone out of my way to keep the man happy. But my relationship with Merle was something else altogether. I can't imagine a tough business type like Douglas Channon ever putting his signature to a contract just for the sake of Merle getting a man she happened to fancy."

"But you were lunching with Merle today," Lee accused him, unable to let go.

"If you'd waited another minute instead of rushing off like that," Jake told her, "you'd have seen her father join us. That's what it was, Lee, a business lunch, pure and simple." He felt for her hand and linked his fingers through hers, their two palms touching warmly. "I want you to understand something, Lee. Since the first moment I set eyes on you, standing there in my cottage like a beautiful apparition, I've not given the least thought to any other woman besides you. Not Merle, nor any other previous girlfriend. Before today I couldn't understand why you were having this extraordinary effect on me, so that I was incapable of working properly. I even got impatient with myself for letting our relationship drive everything else from my mind. But I felt wonderfully happy, wonderfully alive, thinking of you and yearning for you every minute of the day, and dreaming of you at night. I've been obsessed with you, my darling, you and you alone."

"All the same," Lee faltered, "you went to stay at Merle's home last weekend."

"Merle's father's home," he corrected. "She happens to live there, too. And since Douglas Channon had specially set up the weekend for me to meet the manager of a new hotel he's acquiring, I couldn't very well call it off. If you must know, Merle was more than somewhat annoyed at my lack of interest in her. Not that I've ever misled her in any way at all. I've never made any promises about where our relationship was leading. I can only presume that when she came to Aberdyffryn on Monday and happened to hear from one of her eager informants that I had taken you out on *Lancashire Lass* on Saturday, she put two and two together and came up with an answer she didn't very much like. In fact, with feminine intuition, she probably realized that I'd fallen in love with you before I even realized it myself."

Lee was silent, though her heart was beating painfully. A new sort of timidity was making her feel scared. Scared of grasping too eagerly at what she yearned to believe. From out of the murk ahead of them, a pair of headlights approached. The car drew up alongside, and the driver wound his window down.

"Are you okay?" he shouted.

Jake jerked a thumbs-up sign, and the man drove on with a smiling nod, obviously relieved not to be called on to give assistance. Jake asked slowly, "Lee . . . about Ashley Hammond?"

"Ashley is my professional partner," she told him, "and a good friend."

"Yes, but what else is he to you?"

"Nothing else."

Jake hesitated. "Does *he* know that?"

"I've never given him cause to think otherwise."

"Not even . . . I saw you kissing on the esplanade."

"It was a kiss Ashley took, and from my standpoint it was a zero, a meaningless kiss. You even noticed that yourself, Jake."

"It was what I wanted to think," he said slowly.

"Well, you were right."

Jake heaved a long sigh that seemed an amalgam . . . of anxiety, hope, pleading. "It looks as if the two of us are equal as far as other relationships are concerned, Lee."

"Not quite equal," she retorted. "Ashley has at no time been my lover." She paused, and added in a lower voice, "My marriage was a dismal failure, but there's been no one else since my husband was killed. Not until you, Jake."

He took her hand and pressed it. "I'm sorry, darling, for comparing us like that."

"Don't be. I'm not censuring you for what's happened in the past, Jake. I just wanted you to know about me, that's all."

"People talk about love, about making love and being lovers, when they actually mean something quite different," Jake said thoughtfully. "Until I met you, Lee, I'd never made love to a woman in my life . . . not really made love. I tried to fool myself that it was the same with you as with all the others—just better. I refused to see the truth. I love you, darling. I love you with all my heart. You must believe me."

"I want to believe you, Jake . . . oh, I want to so much. But . . . if it weren't really true, if you mean something different than I do by love, I couldn't bear it."

"I love you," he insisted. "Love you in the deepest, truest way there is. I love you in a way I never imagined I should come to feel about another human being. I know now that I want to spend the rest of my life proving my love to you. I want to be with you always, Lee. I want you to be my wife. Just say one word, and you can make me the luckiest man alive."

Even now she hesitated, hardly able to believe in—to trust—such incredible happiness. But when Jake took her into his arms Lee's fears all fled and she melted against him. He was very gentle, very tender . . . and very self-effacing. "I only wish that I deserved you better," he whispered into the silken softness of her hair.

It was this humbling of himself that finally reached through to her and made her sure. "Don't talk like that, Jake. I love you and I want you. Of course I'll marry you, whenever you say."

For long, hypnotic moments they clung together, without passion or urgent desire, just with the relief of discovering their mutual love and feeling the happiness and joy flow warmly between them. Unnoticed, the rain thundered on the car roof as the heavens opened wider and the whole night sky seemed awash. The rumble of thunder, reverberating around the mountains, was like a triumphant drumroll.

Jake kissed her tenderly for the hundredth time, then at last drew back shakily. "Darling Lee, we can't stay here forever."

Lee shook herself out of her dream, and tried to be practical. "Yes, we'd better get back to Aberdyffryn. Will you help me reverse the car?"

"I seem to recall you asking me that once before," he said with a soft chuckle. "But I've got a much better idea. The place where you took the wrong turning that night— or rather, where you took the *right* turning—is only about a mile ahead."

"You mean . . . go to your cottage?"

"Where better, my love? It's where it all began for us, before things became so complicated. You've checked out of your hotel; nobody's expecting you anywhere. And as for me . . . I'm a free agent."

She smiled at him lovingly. "Don't ever say that again, Jake Talbot. I've caught you in my trap, and I intend to keep you firmly tethered."

"It's the only way I want to be, my precious Lee. Come to think of it, this about sums us up, doesn't it . . . cozy and warm together in the car, while outside all hell is breaking loose."

"It will be cozier still at your cottage," she said huskily, enticingly. "Will you drive ahead and lead the way?"

"No fear, I'm not separating from you now, even by the distance between two vehicles. Anyway, you'd have a job driving this small car up that track to my place. It'll be more like a torrential stream by now. No darling, we'll leave your car here. Let me just move it off the road onto the grass verge, and it'll be perfectly safe."

Having done so, he turned to her and asked, "Now, all set to make a mad dash through the rain to my car?"

"There's my luggage, Jake, on the back seat."

"Sure." He jumped out, and before reaching in for the bags he whipped off his jacket so that when Lee emerged he could hold it over her head like a canopy.

"You'll get drenched!" she protested.

"In the best of causes." He locked her car and gathered the bags in his free hand. They sprinted the few yards to the white Mercedes, flinging themselves inside and collapsing together in a laughing, breathless heap. There was the taste of rain on Jake's lips as he kissed her, and his shirt clung to his solid chest like a second skin.

"You mustn't get cold," she said protectively.

"Cold!" He scoffed at the very idea.

Under other circumstances, the journey up the mountain track would have been a miserable, scary experience. Jake kept the big car nosing forward into the streaming blackness, deftly correcting each slide and skid before it really started. Eventually, they lurched to a stop outside the cottage. This time there was no welcoming light from within, but even so it beckoned Lee like a much-loved friend.

When they were safely inside and Jake had switched on lights and an electric heater, they clung together long and lingeringly. Then he knelt before the hearth and built a fire of dry logs that he'd left piled there in readiness. Within a few minutes it was crackling brightly.

Jake peeled off his wet shirt, and his muscled torso gleamed like polished copper in the warm red-and-gold light of the leaping flames. Diffidently, lovingly, Lee reached out a hand and ran her fingertips back and forth across the smooth rippling skin of his shoulders. He shivered and wriggled with pleasure at her touch.

"That feels wonderful!" he breathed.

"I could go on doing it for ever and ever," Lee said dreamily, thrilling to the pulsing, vibrant heat of his body.

"No, there are other and still more wonderful things for us to do." He smiled with a depth of tenderness that made Lee's heart swell with happiness. He leaned and kissed her cheek, drawing her against his side. "But that's what's so marvelous about being in love, isn't it? The way

I feel, I have an urge to strip off your clothes right here and now and possess you greedily in a storm of passion, but then I remind myself of the wonderful fact that we have all the time in the world to be together and make love . . . tonight, tomorrow and every day and week and month and year forevermore."

"We both have to do a spot of work occasionally," she teased, when she'd caught her breath at the dizzying prospect.

"In between times," he granted. "Look, I suggest we both go and get into some dry clothes. Find something in that suitcase of yours that's nice and sexy. Not," he added, running a finger down the length of her spine in an erotic journey of delight, "that I need any encouragement."

"Need it or not, Jake Talbot, encouragement is what you're going to get from me."

"Is that a threat?"

She grinned. "No, it's a promise!"

"I'll hold you to it, you bewitching female."

While Jake went up to his room, Lee slipped into the downstairs bathroom and washed, then she put on the same dress that she'd worn that first evening, of soft, misty-green angora wool. She brushed out her honey-gold hair and left it flowing wild and free in the way he loved so much.

"Do you approve?" she asked, smiling, when she emerged. Jake himself was wearing jeans and a crewneck sweater.

"Approve is far too mild a word to use," he stated, surveying her with an intensity that sent shivers running through her body. "You look fantastic, Lee, and I don't know how I'm going to keep my hands off you."

"Why bother trying?" She laughed shamelessly.

Jake moved swiftly, gathering her into the circle of his

arms. His smoky-brown eyes widened with delight when he realized that she wore nothing beneath the dress.

"This is how you should always be," he murmured thickly, his hands cupping and kneading the soft round- ness of her buttocks. "Beautifully gettable."

"You, though, are much more cluttered up with clothes than I," she pointed out critically.

"Maybe. But I doubt if you'll encounter any insur- mountable difficulties, my love."

The minutes flew by with their caresses until, at Lee's suggestion, they cooled their passion and adjourned to the tiny kitchen to see what they could rustle up for dinner. The larder yielded a variety of cans . . . ham, baked beans, mushrooms. There was coffee, sugar, dried milk and a bag of flour, a bottle of olive oil and a couple of eggs that proved to be still fresh. Jake explained that he always cleared out perishables, never knowing how long before he would be able to get to the cottage again.

"I'll manage to knock up something edible," she assured him.

"You're a genius," he said fondly, bending his head to nibble her neck.

"Say that when you've eaten," she threw back, dodg- ing away from him. But preparing just a simple meal . . . pancakes filled with chopped ham, baked beans and mushrooms, with an artfully concocted sauce poured over . . . took an inordinately long time, because Jake, who was supposed to be setting the table, kept returning to the kitchen to claim a kiss. At last it was done, though.

Carrying in the serving dish, Lee found that he had set places for them side by side. "No," she said firmly. "We'll sit opposite, if you don't mind. We've got things to sort out, you and I, and we'll do it better at a slight distance."

Grumbling, Jake did as she instructed, then picked up a corkscrew and started opening a bottle of wine. "So what's all this serious talk to be about, darling?"

Sitting down, Lee slid a couple of pancakes onto a plate and handed it across to him. "I'm an architect, Jake, and my work means a lot to me. Being married won't change that fact. I'll still want to practice."

"But not with Ashley Hammond, I hope?"

"No, that wouldn't be practicable, and we'll have to formally dissolve our partnership. But I could set up a small office in Aberdyffryn, couldn't I?"

"Good idea. After all, you already have your first client there."

Lee looked at him a little anxiously. "Will it suit you, Jake, to have a business connection with your wife?"

"As long as you don't expect any favors," he said flatly. "I'll still demand a first-class job. But then I know I'll get one, right?"

"Right," she confirmed.

"About Ashley . . ."

"What about him?"

"He'll be pretty annoyed over this, won't he? Losing you as a professional partner, and as a potential romantic interest."

Lee smiled and shook her head. "Ashley is a dear man and he's been very good to me. But he's a level-headed, unemotional sort of person. He's genuinely fond of me, as I am of him, but love doesn't enter into it. Ashley has viewed me for some time as a suitable wife, and finally, when he came to Aberdyffryn last Sunday, he worked 'round to proposing to me. I told him, as gently as I could, that there was no question of it and he still hasn't quite accepted that in his mind. But he will. And when he hears that you and I are going to be married, there'll be no hard feelings and he'll wish us luck."

Jake relaxed. "Then I'll agree to him coming to the wedding."

"Generous of you!"

He brandished his fork at her. "I won't have my wife mocking me."

"But I'm not your wife . . . yet."

"In all but name," he said softly. "You belong to me, Lee . . . body and soul, utterly and completely. And before you mount your feminist high horse, I belong to you in the same way."

Smiling at him, she asked wickedly, "Would you want to invite Merle to the wedding?"

"No way. Not that she'd come."

"Glad I am to hear it," Lee retorted in a strong Welsh lilt. "I'm going to find it mighty hard to be civil to Merle, whenever we happen to meet."

Jake grinned understandingly. "What about her father, though? You and Douglas seemed to get on famously."

"We did." She giggled. "Matter of fact he offered me a contract as architectural consultant to Channon Hotels, with—to use his own words—a nice fat retainer."

"Hey, you didn't tell me that. I thought it was something to do with Nantlys Court."

"That too. The one arose from the other."

"But you turned down his consultancy offer?"

"Flat."

Jake gave her a speculative glance. "I noticed the way Douglas Channon looked at you that day. Was the contract to include a clause you didn't find acceptable?"

"There were no strings—he made that quite specific."

"So the subject did arise?"

In answer, Lee pulled a face at him.

"I'll make a bet with you," Jake went on thoughtfully. "When Douglas hears that you're going to be practicing in Aberdyffryn, he'll renew that offer. Whatever extras he might have had in mind originally, he's shrewd enough to know that he'd be onto a good thing, having you as consultant to Channon Hotels. Douglas can recognize quality when he sees it . . . in women, in architects. Will you accept his offer, Lee?"

"Would you let me?" she queried.

"Could I stop you?"

"We'll talk about it if and when the time comes. Right?"

They smiled lovingly into each other's eyes, enjoying the perfect harmony of understanding. When they'd finished eating, they made coffee and sat together on the sofa in front of the fire. Lee snuggled close against Jake's hard-muscled body, reveling in the warmth that radiated from him, the feel of his fingertips lightly rasping her skin as he endlessly caressed her. She savored the clean male tang of him.

"I love you."

"I love you."

Which of them said it first? It didn't matter. The very air they breathed was redolent of love. Time ceased to have any relevance as the two of them sat on before the fire, exchanging softly murmured words and broken phrases from the depths of their hearts, kissing and touching one another. Then at some given moment, with no prompting but a sudden mutual flare of urgency, they stood up together and feverishly began to remove the restrictive barriers of their clothes. Easing down Lee's dress, Jake disposed of it in a flash, then gave assistance to her trembling fingers to strip himself until both of them stood quite naked, gazing at one another in open adoration, exclaiming in joyous wonder.

"Each time I look at you like this," he said huskily, "I realize that I haven't fully appreciated your beauty before. I could stand and stare at you for hours, my darling, drinking in your loveliness."

"Oh, Jake!"

In a quick gesture that was both timid and brazen, Lee flung herself at him, winding her arms around his neck, leaning against his flesh, slipping one leg between his until she felt totally held and enveloped by him. His parted lips met hers in a hungry, devouring kiss that swept Lee to a glorious height of shuddering passion. She pressed even closer against the length of his virile frame, exulting in the heat of his desire, the insistent throb of his body's need.

Swiftly, taking her by surprise, Jake swept her up into the cradle of his arms, their mouths still sweetly joined, and laid her gently upon the sofa. Kneeling before her with the firelight flickering across the muscled contours of his shoulders, he began a slow, meticulous perusal of her body as if it were unexplored territory to him, yet at the same time belovedly familiar. His two hands molded her shape, reverencing each curve, each hollow, with total, uninhibited freedom. His mouth made its own independent journey, his tongue sometimes softly pliant, sometimes a hard, demanding probe that brought Lee to a state of flooding delight so that she moaned in rapture. Fingers splayed, Jake caressed her legs . . . trailing across the long curve of her thighs, seeking out the delicate formation of her knees, gliding down smooth calves to reach her feet and hold them fondly in his hands.

Her womanhood burned in its need for fulfillment. Still unhurriedly, Jake moved upward again and his lips encircled one of her yearning breasts, the tip of his tongue darting back and forth across the tingling nipple. His hands tantalized her, till she writhed and gasped in thwarted torment, beginning the sublime ascent that was almost frightening in its remembered intensity. With fingertips that moved slowly and rhythmically, he lifted her from plateau to ever-higher plateau to a quivering dependency on him for the ecstasy that he alone could bring her. Her cries and moans of pleasure mingled with the hiss of burning logs, the lashing of the rain outside and Jake's whispered words of love.

"Yes," she sobbed. "Yes, yes . . ." In a final, rapturous explosion, her body jerking convulsively, she was transported into the blissful golden realms he had shown her before.

"My darling!" Jake whispered hoarsely. "Oh, my darling, wonderful, precious Lee."

She looked up at him mistily and her words were blurred by the intoxication of her emotions. "I love you, Jake."

His dark eyes, catching glints of firelight, were very tender. "I shall require proof of that, my darling. Incontrovertible proof."

"You shall have it," she said, reaching her arms out to him and urging his weight upon her.

"It will be a lifetime job," he warned solemnly. "I'm a hard man to convince."

"Then I'd better start without delay."

Jake in his turn shivered and moaned as she touched him with exquisitely sensitive fingers, finally guiding him in the joining of their bodies.

"I shall make love to you all night long," he murmured throatily.

"Promises!"

"And all day long tomorrow."

"What about work?"

Jake uttered an inelegant expletive about work.

"Food?"

"There are farms here in the mountains, trout in the streams. Anyway, who cares about food?"

He thrust more deeply into her, and Lee abandoned herself delightedly to his passion, rejoicing when at last he uttered a ragged, breathless cry, shuddered once more and relapsed into stillness. She kissed him on the lips, and Jake responded by drawing her against him with a contented sigh.

"All night long," he murmured again.

He was a man, she was to discover, who kept his promises.

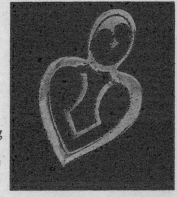

YOU'LL BE SWEPT AWAY WITH SILHOUETTE DESIRE

$1.75 each

1 ☐ James	5 ☐ Baker	8 ☐ Dee
2 ☐ Monet	6 ☐ Mallory	9 ☐ Simms
3 ☐ Clay	7 ☐ St. Claire	10 ☐ Smith
4 ☐ Carey		

$1.95 each

11 ☐ James	29 ☐ Michelle	47 ☐ Michelle	65 ☐ Allison
12 ☐ Palmer	30 ☐ Lind	48 ☐ Powers	66 ☐ Langtry
13 ☐ Wallace	31 ☐ James	49 ☐ James	67 ☐ James
14 ☐ Valley	32 ☐ Clay	50 ☐ Palmer	68 ☐ Browning
15 ☐ Vernon	33 ☐ Powers	51 ☐ Lind	69 ☐ Carey
16 ☐ Major	34 ☐ Milan	52 ☐ Morgan	70 ☐ Victor
17 ☐ Simms	35 ☐ Major	53 ☐ Joyce	71 ☐ Joyce
18 ☐ Ross	36 ☐ Summers	54 ☐ Fulford	72 ☐ Hart
19 ☐ James	37 ☐ James	55 ☐ James	73 ☐ St. Clair
20 ☐ Allison	38 ☐ Douglass	56 ☐ Douglass	74 ☐ Douglass
21 ☐ Baker	39 ☐ Monet	57 ☐ Michelle	75 ☐ McKenna
22 ☐ Durant	40 ☐ Mallory	58 ☐ Mallory	76 ☐ Michelle
23 ☐ Sunshine	41 ☐ St. Claire	59 ☐ Powers	77 ☐ Lowell
24 ☐ Baxter	42 ☐ Stewart	60 ☐ Dennis	78 ☐ Barber
25 ☐ James	43 ☐ Simms	61 ☐ Simms	79 ☐ Simms
26 ☐ Palmer	44 ☐ West	62 ☐ Monet	80 ☐ Palmer
27 ☐ Conrad	45 ☐ Clay	63 ☐ Dee	81 ☐ Kennedy
28 ☐ Lovan	46 ☐ Chance	64 ☐ Milan	82 ☐ Clay

YOU'LL BE SWEPT AWAY WITH SILHOUETTE DESIRE

$1.95 each

83 ☐ Chance	93 ☐ Berk	103 ☐ James	113 ☐ Cresswell
84 ☐ Powers	94 ☐ Robbins	104 ☐ Chase	114 ☐ Ross
85 ☐ James	95 ☐ Summers	105 ☐ Blair	115 ☐ James
86 ☐ Malek	96 ☐ Milan	106 ☐ Michelle	116 ☐ Joyce
87 ☐ Michelle	97 ☐ James	107 ☐ Chance	117 ☐ Powers
88 ☐ Trevor	98 ☐ Joyce	108 ☐ Gladstone	118 ☐ Milan
89 ☐ Ross	99 ☐ Major	109 ☐ Simms	119 ☐ John
90 ☐ Roszel	100 ☐ Howard	110 ☐ Palmer	120 ☐ Clay
91 ☐ Browning	101 ☐ Morgan	111 ☐ Browning	
92 ☐ Carey	102 ☐ Palmer	112 ☐ Nicole	

SILHOUETTE DESIRE, Department SD/6
1230 Avenue of the Americas
New York, NY 10020

Please send me the books I have checked above. I am enclosing $_____
(please add 75¢ to cover postage and handling. NYS and NYC residents please
add appropriate sales tax). Send check or money order—no cash or C.O.D.'s
please. Allow six weeks for delivery.

NAME_____

ADDRESS_____

CITY_____ STATE/ZIP_____

Coming Next Month

Late Rising Moon by Dixie Browning

Larain expected to get control of her life again as manager of Silas Flynt's art gallery. Instead the icy facade she cultivated melted completely as she abandoned herself in Silas' arms.

Without Regrets by Brenda Trent

Despite their vow never to part, Halette and Kale's blissful marriage had shattered. Now, amidst the splendors of the Orient, the old passions flared again, strong and steady, and challenged all their hesitations.

Gypsy Enchantment by Laurie Paige

Keri Thomas had left Louisiana and Reid Beausan to begin her life again in Houston. But on her return, the man who had stolen her innocence seduced her again, rekindling passions she had been desperate to forget.

Color My Dreams by Edith St. George

When cool Robyn Stuart travelled to Fiji to lure artist Philip Holt back to civilization, she didn't expect to be seduced by the primitive pulse of the island—and discover her own primitive passions in the arms of its devastating inhabitant.

Passionate Awakening by Gina Caimi

Arden knew it was a chance in a lifetime when she was commissioned to write the biography of reclusive tycoon Flint Masters. But her objectivity gave way once Flint revealed his most private self to her—and his sudden interest in her as a woman.

Leave Me Never by Suzanne Carey

It was an honor to be accepted as a student under the great Dr. Benjamin Reno. But Terry had to fight her feelings for the man who had claimed her body and soul six years before—and whose eyes now burned with anger as well as passion.